Little Yellow Farm House in Iowa

ISBN 978-1-894666-39-8

Precious Memories:
Book 2: Years Eleven through Seventeen:
World War II Years

Little Yellow Farm House in Iowa

A Fictionalized Biography of
Katherine Vastenhout

Carol Brands

Illustrations by John P. Cady
(johnpcasso@yahoo.com)

INHERITANCE PUBLICATIONS
NEERLANDIA, ALBERTA, CANADA
PELLA, IOWA, U.S.A.

Library of Congress Cataloging-in-Publication Data

Brands, Carol.
  Little yellow farm house in Iowa : a fictionalized biography of Katherine
Vastenhout ; illustrations by John P. Cady / Carol Brands.
      p. cm. — (Precious Memories Book 2: Years Eleven through Seventeen:
World War II Years)
  ISBN 978-1-894666-39-8 (pb)
  1. Vastenhout, Katherine Kroontje—Fiction. 2. Families—Iowa—Fiction.
3. Iowa—History—20th century—Fiction. 4. Biographical fiction. I. Cady,
John P. II. Title.
  PS3602.R3626L58 2012
  813'.6—dc23

                                                                2012036054

Cover Photography by Jill Fennema
with Rachel De Jong at Katherine's Piano

Illustrations by John P. Cady

978-1-894666-39-8

Published by Inheritance Publications
Box 154, Neerlandia, Alberta Canada T0G 1R0
Tel. 780-674-3949
Web site: http://www.telusplanet.net/public/inhpubl/webip/ip.htm
E-Mail inhpubl@telusplanet.net

Published simultaneously in U.S.A. by Inheritance Publications
Box 366, Pella, Iowa 50219

Printed in Canada

* * *

Written in collaboration
with Katherine (Kroontje) Vastenhout
by Carol Brands

Editing and added information
by Dorothy Kroontje Ricehill,
Gerrit Kroontje
and Ruth (Tilstra) Kinkade

Precious Memories

By J.B.F. Wright

Precious memories, how they linger,
How they ever flood my soul!
In the stillness of the midnight,
Precious, sacred scenes unfold.

Precious memories, unseen angels,
Sent from somewhere to my soul;
How they linger, ever near me,
And the sacred past unfold.

In the stillness of the midnight,
Echoes from the past I hear;
Old time singing, gladness bringing,
From that lovely land somewhere.

Chorus
Precious memories, how they linger,
How they ever flood my soul!
In the stillness of the midnight,
Precious, sacred scenes unfold.

Chorus
Precious memories, how they linger,
How they ever flood my soul;
In the stillness of the midnight,
Precious, sacred scenes unfold.

Precious father, loving mother,
Fly across the lonely years;
And old home scenes of my childhood,
In fond memory appear.

As I travel on life's pathway,
Know not what the years may hold;
As I ponder, hope grows fonder,
Precious memories flood my soul.

Chorus
Precious memories, how they linger,
How they ever flood my soul!
In the stillness of the midnight,
Precious, sacred scenes unfold.

Chorus
Precious memories, how they linger,
How they ever flood my soul!
In the stillness of the midnight,
Precious, sacred scenes unfold.

Preface by the Author

Incredible how things can change!

Change . . . so quickly. So unexpectedly. So completely.

In this past year, my life has changed that way. I no longer work at Edgebrook. No longer assist Katherine, my dear "mother", with her cares.

After nearly twelve years as a CNA at Edgebrook Care Center, this phase of my life has ended. God led me to stay more at home with my husband. For extra income, I now clean houses.

But never would Katherine and I abandon the close friendship we have formed over the last years! Never!

We continue to meet with each other bi-weekly. We head out to the Pizza Ranch in Edgerton, or to Lange's in Pipestone, or to Chit Chat's in Luverne . . .

And we rehash memories. Katherine's memories.

Bringing the past back to life so that it can form another book.

The first book we wrote was of the first ten years of Katherine's life. It contains memories forged in the crucible of the toughest years financially, the ten years in Katherine's first tiny home.

This second book is of Katherine's second home, just as tiny as the first home. The Depression was ending yet times were still difficult.

But improving! Always improving! Each year a little easier.

The great distress in this second home was World War II.

Uncle Bill Tilstra, Mama Susie's fiddle-strumming brother from "Inspiration Hills", was in the navy during the war. This united the entire family in the war effort and made Katherine intensely aware of every nuance of the war. She began a scrapbook as a school assignment and continued adding to the scrapbook even after she graduated. It contains hundreds of war clippings.

This second house — and Katherine's second school — were also the last years of Katherine's schooling. Iowa had no busses to bring children to high school and Papa couldn't possibly bring Katherine to town every single day. The luxury of extended education would begin with improved economy and bussing – soon, but not soon enough to benefit Katherine.

With the war going on . . . with her years of education ending . . . yet with the possibility of occasional luxuries, Katherine's life changed during the war years. As she often said, children grew up quickly.

Katherine's family lived in their second tiny home for seven years.

Let's join Katherine and see how God led in those years . . .

Carol Brands, friend of Katherine

Katherine in 1941 at age ten

Dedication

Willie lived his retirement years in Texas, where his heart gave out in 2008.
That made Katherine the oldest of five living family members as we wrote this book.
I thank Katherine's family for incredible support.
Dorothy took Katherine's place as family historian.
Gerrit and Harriet provided invaluable input on the war and Chapter 10.
We thank Bill Tilstra's daughter, Ruth Kinkade, for an enjoyable and
informative day at her alpaca farm near Hutchinson, Minnesota.

To both Katherine's and my extended families, this book is dedicated with love.

From my family:

Daryl and Cathy, and son James, thanks for our tenth grandchild, our first
granddaughter, born on April 3, 2012. What a blessing!

Kristin and Phillip, God enhanced your lives – and ours – with four little sons.
Your lives touch many lives, including ours.

Jonathan, we are grateful to sleep at your home when we visit Michigan.
Keep studying! May God bless you with a meaningful life of service.

Alyssa and Bob and four children: Your life has seen so many recent changes.
May God bless your move to North Dakota. We love having you closer to home.

Shawn and Jeremy, my tall younger sons, so different from each other:
God walk with you, Shawn, as you have finished college and seek a permanent job.
And with you, Jeremy, back from your years in the navy, entering college.
These early adult years are so critical. We pray for you every day.

Monica, you have now graduated from four years of college. Congratulations
on your own first published book! Thanks for being the special person you are.

Tricia, as I wrote this book, it brightened my day when you entered the door.
Now that you live in Rapid City, you provide a place to visit – but we miss you!

Harold, you remain as the children take wing.

Thank you for being here through the changes of past years.
Thanks for patience when I stay up and type half the night!

And finally, Father in heaven, my Savior and my Lord: thanks for everything.
Thanks for the wealth of these people in my life. Thanks for opportunity to write.
It makes me feel small, Father. It's all Thine. All of it!

Family Tree of Katherine Kroontje (Vastenhout)

Wilbur Kroontje—m. on February 16, 1927 to—Susie Tilstra
11/29/1899   **10/26/1903**

1. *Son* **Wiebe Jan (William or Willie) Kroontje 04/10/1928**

2. *Daughter* **Katherine Kroontje (Vastenhout) 06/03/1930**

3. *Son* **Gerrit Kroontje 05/22//1933**

4. *Daughter* **Dorothy Kroontje (Ricehill) 07/29/1934**

5. *Stillborn Infant Son* **02/23/1936**

6. *Son* **John Cecil Kroontje 02/22/1941**

7. *Son* **Marvin Walter Kroontje 05/04/1942**

Precious Memories:
Book 2: Years Eleven through Seventeen: World War II Years

Little Yellow Farm House in Iowa

Table of Contents

PART 1: 1941 – 1942

First Years

in the Little Yellow House

. . .

and

. . .

Entering the War

"Home, home, sweet, sweet home!
Be it ever so humble, there's no place like home."

Chapter 1. January, 1941 Part I

The Upsetting Move

"No! No! I won't go!"

"Katherine, Honey, we don't have a choice," Mama's reasonable voice chided. "This farm doesn't belong to us. The landlord needs it now for his son."

"But that's mean! He shouldn't move us off our farm! I've lived here for ten years now. We've worked and worked and improved the whole farm. Now he wants it back again. It's not fair!"

"Child, I know this is the only home you've known. It's the only farm your father and I have had since our marriage, fourteen years ago. But you will see. We can make a home of another farm, too. We will!"

"But it'll mean going to a whole new school! I love my school! I love Miss Sands . . . and all my friends," Katherine sobbed. "Especially Jessie."

"Honey, life is life. We have to do what we have to do.

"And remember," Mama added, "God is in control. Nothing happens by chance. He will turn it for our good. Believe that."

Katherine knew it was useless to say more. The owner really was a nice man. His son was getting married and he simply needed his farm back now.

She was still heartbroken. She loved every cranny on this farm . . .

*   *   *

The farm Papa had found to move onto was an adjacent farm, just north of the farm they had lived on for ten years. Although the farm was next to the first one, the houses were nearly two miles apart because of their locations.

The new farm would have cheaper rent than the first farm, since it was run down. That meant more work fixing things up but it was worth it due to cheaper rent.

It was a bad time of year to be moving. Usually, moving time in Iowa was in March. Lots of rentals ended then. This was January of 1941, a blustery winter month. Things had never warmed up much since the Armistice Day Blizzard of 1940, only two months ago. There were snow banks everywhere. Who would choose to move in frigid January?

At least the car in the garage wasn't snowed-in anymore!

And at least all the buildings were now shoveled out.

Katherine was old enough to understand some things. She counted them:

Finger One: it took money to buy a farm. Papa never owned his own farm.

Finger Two: Mama was going to have another baby in February. After five years without a baby, Mama had to be very careful with this pregnancy.

Finger Three: Papa and Mama wanted to move before the baby was born.

Finger Four: this would mean even more work than usual. Both before and after school, they would be busy, busy, busy . . .

And why? So things would improve? No way!

But it had to be. So Katherine choked back her tears and decided she wouldn't cry again. She must help Mama all she could to make it easier.

*   *   *

As Papa drove up to the "new" house with Mama and her, Katherine sat on the front seat, straining to see.

The new house was a drab yellow. Yellow! Houses were supposed to be white, not yellow. Every other house in the neighborhood was white. Yuck!

Some things about the houses were similar, Katherine decided. Both houses had two porches — on both houses, the front porch was enclosed. In both houses, from the front porch you walked into the kitchen and the kitchen was the width of the house, a main room to be lived in. And both houses had just three small rooms for the downstairs with a fixed-up attic for an upstairs. Small. Both houses were small.

Very small! Far too small for a family soon to have five children!

Mama wanted things done in the new house. *Before* moving, it must be cleaned. *After* moving, it must be wall-papered.

"We will be having visitors after the baby is born," Mama had said. "We must have everything ready for company."

*   *   *

Housecleaning was hard work for a ten-year-old girl. Katherine was used to hard work but this used new muscles. It was a challenge.

"Mama," Katherine asked as she scrubbed the baseboards, "where will you put things in this kitchen?"

"Well, see by the outside wall? This kitchen has a well — a cistern — right outside the kitchen, under the enclosed porch. That should make it easier to wash dishes, yes? The dishpan is on the corner cupboard near the porch.

"Across from the dishpan counter, in the other corner, is the stairway to upstairs. Next to that is the food pantry. We never had a pantry in the old house.

"The table and chairs, of course, will be in the center.

"On the wall, left of the dishpan counter, will be the corn cob stove.

"On the opposite side of the kitchen, by the door to the open porch, will be two things: a cupboard for dishes and the small table with the radio."

"Oh!" exclaimed Katherine, her face lighting up. "We'll still have the radio in the kitchen? I'm glad of that!"

Katherine recalled when Papa had installed the radio. It had changed their home. Ever since its purchase, there had been music and programs to listen to in spare time or when working in the kitchen.

"Yes," agreed Papa, who was listening as he washed walls for Mama. "We are all thankful for that radio, right? It has cheered up many a dreary day!"

*   *   *

"This house has another thing that you will appreciate in the summer, Katherine," Papa now said. "It has a summer kitchen."

"What's a summer kitchen?" Katherine questioned.

"Look through the kitchen door, past the porch. Do you see that small building to the left? That's a summer kitchen."

"So, in the summer we won't use this kitchen?"

Mama laughed, almost gleefully.

"That's the idea! Won't it be wonderful to keep the heat of cooking out of the house? We'll butcher, cook, render lard, and even do laundry out there, so the house doesn't get so roasting hot. Doesn't that make you happy?"

Katherine still didn't want to move. But the summer kitchen would be nice, very nice, in the heat of summer.

*   *   *

Papa worked while the children were in school. Katherine was surprised how quickly he cleaned the ceilings and woodwork. It felt funny, though, running through an empty house. Everything echoed — like a ghost house.

Papa spent one whole afternoon fixing a broken window between the kitchen and the enclosed porch. Even though the porch was enclosed it was not heated, so if the window wasn't fixed the whole house would freeze.

The dining room was no larger than their old dining room. A wall from the stairway and from the kitchen pantry jutted into it on the left. Next to that was the coal burning stove. Papa's bookcase-desk was near the bedroom doorway. In the center of the room was the large, round, oak, company table. The room contained only the stove, desk, and round table.

Later Papa would buy a couch and another surprise for that room. The surprise will be another chapter, a story all by itself.

There were three doorways in the dining room. The first came from the kitchen. To the right was a doorway to the open porch. Across from the kitchen doorway was the bedroom doorway.

"*More doorways than space in the room,*" thought Katherine.

Katherine loved the dining room's oak table. It had four sturdy, swirled legs under it. Although her parents bought it secondhand before she was born, it was a well-built, solid table. Katherine later inherited that table, used it until she sold her final home, and then sold it to a niece.

The third room downstairs was her parents' bedroom. It held only necessary things. At its left end was a curtained closet, Papa and Mama's bed . . . and a chamber pot, of course. Under the single window in the center was the mirrored dresser. On the right would be the baby's crib and wardrobe.

Only one word would describe this room: crowded!

*   *   *

Within one week the yellow house was cleaned and the window fixed. Now it was time to move.

Time to leave the little white house . . .

The only home Katherine had ever known.

> "Be strong and of good courage . . .
> The LORD thy God doth go with thee!"

Authors' sketch of the first floor
of the crowded yellow house.

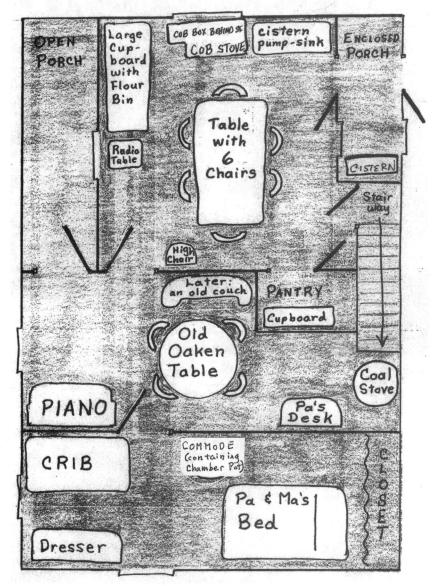

Chapter 2. January, 1941 Part 2

Moving Day

Moving Day was Saturday. Moving would make Mama tired because of the baby . . . but she had Sunday to rest. So Saturday was best.

Mama had begun packing things in boxes as soon as they knew about the move. Papa and she had taken down the pot-bellied stove in the dining room the day before. That meant the dining room was cold on Friday night.

The whole family had to be up long before daylight on moving day. Willie, Katherine, and Gerrit helped outside with barn chores. Then Willie and Gerrit helped Papa empty out farm buildings and line up farm things outside while Katherine and Dorothy helped inside the house, getting last things packed.

They would come back next week and clean the whole house. They didn't want the new owners to complain that they had left it dirty!

*   *   *

"Mama, look, is that the Smidstra's horses and hayrack?"

Katherine hadn't realized that neighbors would be helping. She should have known. Neighbors always helped with big events.

She was excited to see the Smidstras arriving. She ran to meet Jessie. Just one year older than Katherine, Jessie had helped her so much in school. How she would miss her!

Friends made work much more fun. Now it was fun to load boxes into cars and wagons. Papa and the men joked while dismantling stoves. She and Jessie talked as they worked.

Jessie's two older sisters, Jennie and Susie, also helped them move. Jennie often helped Mama. She was already out of grade school when Katherine began first grade.

It took all morning to get the household things moved to the new place. While ladies and children ran back and forth with boxes and boxes of household items, men moved heavy objects. Papa used his own horses and hayrack and they loaded the neighbors' hayracks and wagons.

As soon as Papa and the men took out the kitchen stove, they headed for the new house to install it as well as the dining room pot-bellied stove. Else they would freeze while they worked.

By noon, Katherine couldn't believe the work that had been done. Stoves were hooked up and heating the yellow house. All large furniture was already moved in, beds were set up, kitchen and dining room tables in place.

*   *   *

Katherine's stomach rumbled. Oh, my! They had been so busy moving, what would they do for food? The food was still packed in boxes!

"Ahoy, neighbors! Anyone hungry?"

It was Alice Folkens. A smile spread over Katherine's face. What was she thinking? Of course, neighbors would bring food! They knew Mama was expecting a baby and would want to make it easier for her. Besides, Mr. Folkens and their son Arent, Willie's friend, were already helping Papa.

Minutes later Mrs. Smidstra and Mrs. Eihausen also arrived — with even more food!

It was wonderful. There were sandwiches and desserts, because each neighbor lady had brought her share. In fact, the three ladies insisted Mama keep the extra food for the family's supper.

*   *   *

After dinner, Papa, the hired man, and the neighboring men went back to the first farmstead to move all the livestock to the new farmstead. Papa took Willie and Gerrit to catch the chickens and put them into crates in one wagon. The men chased pigs into another wagon.

Two horses were needed to pull the wagons. The men first went to the far pasture of the old place to get the most reliable horses.

The most reliable horse, of course, was Prince — the horse who had saved two-year-old Dorothy's life at oat threshing time. Katherine still remembered how Dorothy had headed for the sand piles the horses made and how Prince had stopped the entire process, standing with one leg protecting Dorothy. Along with Prince, Papa chose Molly. Both horses would wait quietly while Papa was busy, wouldn't spook, and were strong enough to pull whatever needed pulling.

It was important that the horses should not spook that day. They were going to be helping with pigs . . . and pigs could squeal loudly with almost no reason to squeal. Katherine hated to think how they might squeal when Papa herded them into the wagon to be moved.

And that's exactly what they did, Papa told her later. The pigs squealed "bloody murder" when the men chased them into the wagon. They needed a wagon with good height to the sides to hold the pigs in. The pigs not only squealed, but stood with their legs up the wagon sides, trying to scramble right over and out. My, had they succeeded, they could have killed themselves!

It took about an hour to move the pigs. Prince and Molly were turned into the pasture of the new farm. Then the men returned to the old farm for the other two horses, the cows, and the beef cattle in the far pasture.

*   *   *

The rest of the horses and cattle weren't hard to move. Since the "new" farm was straight north from the old one, there wasn't even a road between them, just a fence.

The "fence" was really just a wire strung between posts. One farmer went to the post and twisted the wires loose. As he pulled away the wire, the fence was gone. Other men surrounded the animals and chased them. Watchie, the dog, was there, too. He had an instinctive ability to herd cattle, guiding them into the next pasture by giving a gentle nip to their heels whenever they stopped to dawdle.

It helped that Prince and Molly were already in the new pasture. Seeing them assured the cattle that they could go there too. As soon as all the cattle were in the new pasture, the wire was quickly replaced so they wouldn't return to the old pasture.

The men's work of moving the animals was finished in a few hours. Then the neighbor farmers stopped by the house for one last cup of coffee before heading to their own homes.

*   *   *

Mrs. Folkens, Mrs. Eihausen, and Mrs. Smidstra went back home right after lunch. They knew Mama needed the afternoon to unpack boxes. And they had to get their own homes ready for Sunday.

Jennie and Jessie stayed to help. They were almost family. And maybe Mama understood how Katherine needed to know Jessie was still her friend. Katherine and Dorothy, Jennie and Jessie, were all in the house to help Mama.

Each emptied box was a success story. One box held food for the food cabinet. An achievement! That cabinet was finished. Other boxes held dishes and silverware, pots and pans — soon in place. Another achievement! On and on it went through the next few hours.

By the time the men — including Willie and Arent — came in for mid-afternoon coffee, telling how it had gone with moving animals, everything downstairs was organized. Papa was surprised and pleased.

The upstairs was still a huge mess. Boxes everywhere. They had to step over boxes to get to the beds. That would be finished next week.

Katherine heaved a sigh of relief. She grabbed Jessie's hands and together they did a little dance.

"We're finished, Jessie! Everything downstairs is in place."

*　　*　　*

Jessie's response was to break into tears.

"Yes, but now I must go home, Katherine. And Monday, you won't be in school anymore. I will miss you so much!"

Tears also in her eyes, Katherine hugged Jessie. "We must pledge never to forget each other, Jessie. Promise me you'll never forget me?"

"How could I forget? You're my best friend!"

"Remember, though, I only live across the road, down three miles. You can visit anytime, right?"

"Before I go home, why don't we sing one last time that song we learned from our *Red Book* in school? Our song to each other?"

Both girls loved singing. Now, together, they sang the old favorite:

Should auld acquaintance be forgot and never bro't to mind?
Should auld acquaintance be forgot and days of auld lang syne?
And here's my hand, my trusty friend, and gie's a hand o' thine,
We'll tak' a cup o' kindness yet, for auld lang syne.

"I never will forget you, Jessie. Will you visit often? Promise?"
Holding hands, the two promised.

And although Katherine and Jessie now attended different schools, the two families remained friends, visiting back and forth and helping each other whenever there was a need. The promise was never broken.

"The storms we so much dread . . .
Break in blessing on our head."

This is the authors' sketch – many, many years later --
of the layout of the attic upstairs of the yellow house.
It was actually more crowded than it looks on this sketch.
And the crawl closet may have been much shorter.
The squiggly-looking walls were really curtains.

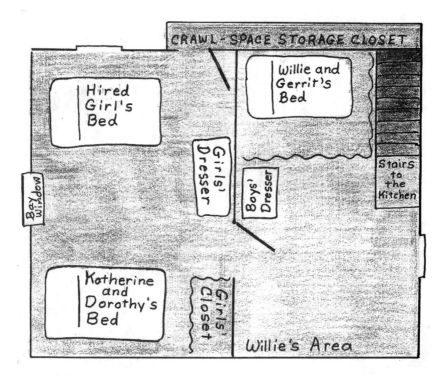

Chapter 3. February, 1941

Month of Three Surprises

I

On Monday, Katherine dragged herself home from school. Every muscle ached from all the work of moving on Saturday.

How she missed her old school!

She knew there was no choice. Iowa schools were set up with a one room school every four square miles — so children could walk to school if the weather wasn't too bad. It was a convenient setup.

Her parents had only moved two miles. From the little white house to the little yellow house. But that was enough to force her to attend a new school. It was enough to upset her life. It would take time — and new friendships — for this wound to heal.

*   *   *

Entering the kitchen from the open porch, Katherine stopped and listened. Neither parent was in sight. From upstairs, she heard scraping noises. What was going on?

Suddenly energized, Katherine ran for the stairs, books still in her arms.

The upstairs had two sections, a boys' half and a girls' half, each with one window. The boys' window was right above the stairs to the left, in the open section of the boys' area with the boys' wardrobe — a section which would become "Willie's domain." It also was the only light to the boys' bed, curtained off at the right.

Beyond the boys' half of the upstairs was the only wall upstairs. A doorway led into the girls' north room — Katherine's room.

It was a finished room, but, like any attic, the ceiling had the same slope as the roof above it. It sloped down to the left by Willie's area. It sloped down to the right by the boys' bed. In Katherine's room, a full half of the upstairs, it stretched up from the left side and then down on the right side. You could only stand tall in the center of the room.

Katherine headed for her room. What was going on in there?

*　　*　　*

"Mama! Papa! What have you been doing?"

Standing in her doorway, Katherine stared in surprise. How her room had changed that day while she was in school!

Mama smiled. She looked mighty pleased.

"We wanted to fix up your room, also, Katherine, before the baby is born. After all, this is where Jennie, our hired girl, will sleep."

Katherine knew that the Smidstras' cousin, Jennie Kracht, would help Mama for a few weeks after the baby's birth. But Katherine hadn't expected all the changes.

The room held two full-sized metal beds, one on the left side and one on the right. Both were painted white. There was no mattress on the second one yet. Quilted spreads on both beds were familiar from the old house and, oh, so cozy.

Between the two beds was the bay window. It had been painted white. Katherine loved that window instantly. She had set her special things on it.

By the inside wall on the right was the room's only wardrobe dresser. It was also painted white to match the beds and window. White! White! White!

And on the inside wall on the left, a feed sack curtain had been hung to make a closet for their hanging clothes. Guess what? It was white, too!

Papa pointed to the bed with no mattress.

"We answered an ad for two secondhand store mattresses," he said proudly. "You won't have a corn husk mattress anymore, Young Lady!"

"When we go to get those mattresses, I'll also buy little decals with roses on them," Mama said. "That'll decorate your beds and dresser, and make everything match. Your room will look like a catalogue room."

Katherine was so delighted that she dropped her books on the bed and ran to Mama. Stretching her short arms around Mama's huge girth, she hugged her for all she was worth. She needed no words.

Later, she realized that Mama was trying to help her adjust to the difficult move. She wanted Katherine to see improvements.

II

"I say it's a boy!" Squirt, went a stream of milk into Willie's pail.

"No way, it's a girl!" Squirt, went a stream of milk into Katherine's pail.

Back and forth the teasing went.

Willie and Katherine, Gerrit and Dorothy had all been shooed out to the barn when they returned from school. Willie and Katherine had known for a good while that Mama was "expecting," so they understood that a baby was being born that day. Gerrit and Dorothy hadn't figured out anything.

"What are you two talking about?" demanded seven-year-old Gerrit. "Is someone coming to visit? A boy or a girl?"

"Silly!" teased Willie, winking at Katherine. "You'll know soon enough."

"Well, if you aren't going to tell us, then quit talking in front of us," Gerrit responded, eyebrows lowered with hurt.

"Okay, we'll quit teasing," answered Willie, as he squirted a stream of milk into the waiting mouth of a nearby cat. He didn't waste even a drop.

*   *   *

The children finished the outdoor chores. The February wind howled around the barn. It was suppertime. How long must they wait?

Dorothy, still only six years old, had fallen asleep on a hay bale. Katherine began to look around for something to eat. They had been working ever since school ended . . . and their stomachs were hungry.

It was taking awfully long. Was Mama okay?

Just as Katherine's stomach gave a loud belch of hunger, Willie shouted, "There's a flashlight! Papa's crossing the yard. Hurray!"

All the children ran to the barn door. What did he have to tell them?

*   *   *

"Come, Children, come in the house," Papa's cheerful voice boomed. "I have someone for you to meet."

"Who, Papa?" asked Dorothy, rubbing the sleep from her eyes. "I saw you get Jennie Kracht. Is she visiting?"

Papa tweaked Dorothy's nose and rubbed his hand on her hair.

"Jennie made us supper today. Wasn't that nice of her?"

"Why?" exclaimed Gerrit. "Why'd she make supper?"

"Well, Mama has been in bed all day while you children were in school. We asked Jennie to help Mama, so she made supper. Wasn't that nice?"

Katherine's stomach thought that was okay. She had thought she'd have to fix supper yet!

*   *   *

Papa led the four wide-eyed children through the porch, kitchen, dining room . . . to the bedroom. He looked as proud as a peacock.

Willie and Katherine were not surprised by all the people in the house. They had seen the same kind of visitors when Gerrit and Dorothy were born. But this was new to Gerrit and Dorothy.

"Children, come look at what the doctor brought," Papa said very formally as they entered the bedroom doorway.

Mama was in bed. But she didn't look sick. She was smiling.

Young Dorothy gained her equilibrium first. She ran over to Mama.

"Mama! What are you holding? A . . . a baby?" Her eyes grew wide.

"Oh!" exclaimed Gerrit, suddenly comprehending everything, including Willie's teasing in the barn. "So that's why you were stitching all those baby clothes when you didn't know we were watching. And that's why Willie and Katherine were guessing whether it was a boy or a girl, too, huh?

"Why so secretive? Why couldn't you tell us?" Gerrit accused them.

Katherine ignored Gerrit as she, too, bent over the bed to see the newcomer. "A boy!" she whispered. "Another boy! Oh, look at that cute little nose. Mama, I think he's looking at me. Can he see me?"

"Yes, children, it's another boy. We now have three living sons and two living daughters. God has been good to us, don't you think?"

"What's his name?" asked Willie.

"John. John Cecil Kroontje. Born on February 22, 1941."

"February 22," mused Katherine. "George Washington's birthday."

"Okay, Children," boomed Papa's voice from behind them. "Now that you've seen the new baby, it's time to let your mother rest. Ready for supper?"

*   *   *

At school the next day, everyone talked about the new baby. Teacher let them tell all the details: how they'd waited in the barn; how they'd had supper with Jennie, Dr. Corcran, and the minister; how cute the baby was; how he was born on Washington's birthday.

"A baby's birth is a wonder," the teacher finally ended the children's excitement. "Each child is a miracle. Each of you," she said pointedly, looking around the room. "Each one of you is a blessing, loved by your parents."

Katherine liked that. Maybe this school would be all right, after all.

III

It had been a difficult day for Katherine at school. All day her mind had replayed a scene from a week ago.

That day, Katherine had been helping Mama when Papa had come home with a fairly good-sized box. He was humming as he walked through the door.

"Katherine, come see what I have!" he had called.

To Katherine's astonishment, Papa had an accordion. No one could play it — yet there it was, an accordion!

Papa wanted music in his home. He loved music and played a harmonica himself. He was hoping Katherine could learn to play the accordion.

Delighted, Katherine spent a few hours tinkering with the accordion. But she discovered that a small accordion won't play most songs. She had told Papa that she'd love to learn to play the accordion but it must be a larger size.

Papa nodded. He would return this one and buy a larger one.

But then Mama interfered. She disapproved.

"Such a foolish waste of money!" Mama exclaimed. "What you need to buy for Katherine is a hope chest. Time flies and soon she will need all the things which go in a hope chest. She must begin sewing things now."

Papa looked disappointed but agreed. A new accordion was a lot of money. So he returned the small accordion and bought Katherine a chest of silverware instead, which she could slide under her bed for now. Four years later, he bought her a "hope chest" to keep it in. Thoughts of marriage seemed far, far away yet. But a hope chest took years to build up.

Silverware instead of music?

Katherine had seen Papa's disappointment. And she felt her own just as strongly. How could Mama not understand their need for music?

*   *   *

A strange pickup in their driveway? What on earth . . .

It was the last day of February. Little John Cecil slept most of the time. Jennie, the hired girl, still helped Mama during the day and slept in the girls' room at night. Mama seemed much peppier now.

Walking home, the four school children saw a Ford pickup parked next to the yellow house. Katherine was immediately curious. Dorothy ran straight into the house to see what it meant.

Mama sat at the table feeding John Cecil. Jennie set out snacks for the children. But Papa and two other men were in the dining room. They were pushing a large object on wheels, covered with a dark cloth.

What was under that dark cloth? A new wardrobe?

Papa and the men discussed where to put it.

"I think there," said Papa, pointing past the table to the right corner by the north window. "What do you think, Mama?"

Mama nodded. "That would be good, Wilbur."

Then Mama said firmly, "Now, shut the door, Willie. After the men leave, we'll talk about our new piece of furniture."

*   *   *

The men came back out while the children were munching cookies and drinking fresh milk. One man winked at Katherine before he exited the doorway. Katherine blushed, wondering why he winked at her.

Papa came back into the kitchen and again shut the door.

"Not now," he said firmly. "After chores and supper . . .

"But I'll say this," he added with a smile, looking straight at Katherine, "it's something that is going to be wonderful for our home!"

*   *   *

Chores were finished. Never had the children rushed so fast.

Supper was finished. Katherine had almost choked on her food. Papa reached for the Bible. "*Psalm 150* tonight," he said solemnly.

"*Praise ye the* LORD! . . .
Praise Him according to His excellent greatness . . .
Praise Him with stringed instruments and organs . . .
Let everything that hath breath praise the LORD!"

Papa looked seriously around the table. A twinkle lit his eye, however, as he looked at Katherine. "Why is everyone looking at me?" she wondered.

"As you know, we made a new purchase today," Papa began. "We found a good deal on something we wanted for a long time. We could not turn it down.

"I want you to know that someone in this family has earned it." Again, Papa was looking at Katherine. "She earned it by trying her best in school all the time. Her teachers have told us she should have it.

"All of our family loves music," he continued. "But Katherine" — Papa cleared his throat — "Katherine especially. So, when this piano came for sale . . ."

Papa got no further. Katherine jumped up, squealing with joy. "Papa! You bought a *piano*? Can I have a real teacher and learn to play?"

Papa held his hands up in surrender.

"Yes, yes, Katherine. It's a *real* piano. You'll take *real* lessons. Okay?"

They all rushed then to see that wonderful instrument. It was tall with beautiful scrolls on dark wood. It was magnificent. Katherine's heart pounded. She couldn't wait to touch those white ivories. To think she could learn to play!

Katherine kept that piano all her life, even after marriage. Even after retirement. It moved with her from home to home.

Never again would Katherine regret the move to the second house.

Now they had a radio *and a piano*!

"The Godly woman . . . strengtheneth her arms"

Chapter 4. April 10, 1941 Part 1

Spring Break ??

"Katherine Kroontje! Look what you did!"
Katherine's eyes were wide with horror.
Had she ruined everything?

*   *   *

John Cecil Kroontje had been born six weeks ago. For a month, Jennie Kracht had been at the house every day, helping Mama with housework while Mama regained her strength. Little by little, Mama was getting stronger.

In those days, doctors told mothers to stay in bed for ten days after a baby's birth. If mothers did too much work, it could cause hemorrhaging. Doctors weren't sure how much was too much, so they played it safe: ten days. By the time the ten days were up, Mama could feel herself getting weak. She was thrilled when the ten days were over. She could work again!

Before they became busy with gardening and summer work, she had things to get done in this "new" house.

*   *   *

Every year over Good Friday and Easter, the school had a few days of vacation. It was called Spring Vacation . . . half a week of freedom.

Easter Sunday in 1941 came on April 13. Willie and Katherine, Gerrit and Dorothy all looked forward to the week of vacation.

That was before Katherine knew what Mama had planned.

She wished Jennie were still there helping Mama!

*   *   *

Spring Vacation began on Thursday and lasted through Monday.

The day before Spring Vacation, Papa took Mama to town. Due to John Cecil's birth, money was tight. But Mama squeezed out money for something she thought important.

She wanted wallpaper.

Even though the walls of the new house had been washed, they were ugly. The old wallpaper was faded, smudged, and scratched. It was depressing.

Mama could afford only thin wallpaper. Thin wallpaper was hard to work with. But if you were very, very careful, you could still make an attractive wall.

Mama wanted to wallpaper the kitchen and dining room right away. Visitors would see those two rooms. Mama expected relatives to come see the new baby on Easter Sunday.

So Mama bought enough rolls of thin wallpaper for two rooms . . .

. . . And suddenly Spring Vacation was no vacation at all!

*   *   *

Katherine would be eleven years old in June. She was expected to help with hard jobs. Dorothy, four years younger, was expected to help with smaller jobs. She could gather eggs and watch Baby John.

Since Mama was still regaining strength, she would organize things, make supper, and help as possible. Heavier work had to be done by Katherine.

But Katherine was not yet eleven years old . . .

*   *   *

"Time to get up, Katherine!"

It was early morning, dark outside. Katherine was used to getting up early . . . but she was so sleepy yet. Didn't a vacation mean rest?

"If we are going to paper those walls, Katherine, we must get busy. I want to get the kitchen wallpapered today and the dining room wallpapered tomorrow. We must work hard, right?"

Katherine had never wallpapered before. In the first little white house, she hadn't been born yet when Papa and Mama had done the wallpapering, thirteen years ago. So she was excited about this project.

To think that now she was old enough to help! That felt important.

Yes, Katherine was willing to help. She couldn't wait to see the results.

*   *   *

Walls in Iowa in those days were not wallboard like today. Nor were they wood, but plaster. Plaster was, Katherine thought, horrible stuff. Hard to work with. Chips and little holes had to be filled in before wallpapering was begun.

To fill in a hole, Katherine dipped crumpled newspaper into paste. She pressed the drippy news-ball into the hole to fill it. Then she took a bit of muslin to cover the hole. It had to be as smooth as possible.

If the wall wasn't smooth, then the wallpaper wouldn't be smooth, either.

*   *   *

Mama had a large bucket to make dry paste. She showed Katherine how to mix flour, skimmed milk, and vinegar to make paste. It was hard to stir. Katherine stirred the stiff mixture until it was smooth and goopy. After that, she brushed it gently onto the back of the wall paper.

Old newspapers were spread all over the floor so the goopy paste wouldn't stick to the floor. If goop got on newsprint, it could be thrown away. Katherine would get new newspapers to replace the ruined ones.

*   *   *

"We can be thankful wallpaper is available, Katherine," Mama said as they worked. "You can see how useful it is to cover ugly walls and cracks like we have in this house. Ugly walls become attractive walls."

"How long has wallpaper been around, Mama?" asked Katherine.

"Well, I don't know its whole history," Mama responded with a little laugh. "I think for rich people it's been around for centuries. My mother had wallpaper before I married. Before that it was too expensive."

Mama then laughed again.

"I think by the time you get married, Katherine . . ."

"Mama!" interrupted Katherine. "I'm only ten years old!"

"Yep, but that will change," responded Mama. "What I'm saying is that by then wallpaper will improve. Everything is improving rapidly these days."

"Do you think the paste is stirred enough?" asked Katherine. Her arms hurt already — and they had hardly started!

"Yes, it looks smooth," answered Mama. "Now we have to use it quickly before it dries."

*   *   *

Papa and Willie had finished milking. After they helped themselves to oatmeal with fresh milk, Willie and Gerrit went back outside for other chores while Papa stayed inside to help wallpaper. Since Katherine was too short to reach up to the ceiling, they needed Papa's hands for that job.

*   *   *

The walls of this yellow house had old, scratched-up wood reaching from the floor to halfway up the wall.

"Mama, we can't wallpaper this old wood, can we?" asked Katherine.

"This wood, Katherine, is called *wainscoting*," Mama replied. "Rich people sometimes have all of their walls done in wainscoting. After we finish wallpapering, we will paint the wainscoting a soft white color.

"Right now, we will wallpaper the *upper* half of the walls and the ceiling.

"We'll do the ceiling first," continued Mama. "It's harder to do, easier to make mistakes. Learn this, Katherine: always do the hardest jobs first!"

*   *   *

Mama was right. Doing the ceiling was awfully hard work!

A roll of wallpaper was 1½ feet wide, 30 feet long. Mama cut the wallpaper into strips longer than the width of the room. The room's width was about nine feet but wasn't always the same, so Mama cut extra to make sure each strip was long enough. One wallpaper roll made three strips.

Katherine laid the wallpaper strips upside down on the floor. Using a brush, she spread the paste smoothly on its back side.

Papa took the center board of the kitchen table and laid it across two chairs. Papa and Katherine both had to stand on that board to get the wallpaper stretched across the ceiling. Katherine stood on one end of the board, reaching up with both arms to hold the wallpaper as high as she could reach. Mama stood on the floor on the opposite side of the room, using a broom to hold up her end.

Papa walked back and forth, back and forth on the table board, pressing the ceiling paper tight to the ceiling. He had to make sure all the air bubbles were pressed out and the paper stuck firmly in place. His arms soon became tired.

Katherine's arms became tired, too. It was strenuous work to hold her arms up, up, up for such long periods of time. It was music to her ears when she heard Papa say, "All right, you can step down for a minute now. I'll finish."

Then she got a break.

Papa got the next break. He swung his arms to get circulation back in them while Katherine and Mama spread paste onto the next strip of paper.

*   *   *

Wallpapering wasn't much different from pasting something onto paper at school . . . except that the ceiling was so large and wallpaper so hard to hold up.

. . . And except that wallpaper wrinkled so easily.

It was exciting to see the first strip of wallpaper hung across the ceiling. Papa pressed it over and over to get out every air bubble.

They needed to rest a minute before tackling the next strip.

"A merry heart doeth good like a medicine."

Chapter 5. April 10, 1941 Part 2

The Horrid Hole

One strip: 1 ½ feet of ceiling covered. Two strips: 3 feet covered. Three strips: 4 ½ feet covered. Eight strips: 12 feet covered. Nine strips: this was the last strip of ceiling. Now it was time for a break.

It had taken all morning to do the kitchen ceiling.

"Oh, Mama," moaned Katherine, "my arms are killing me. Do we have to do the whole room today?"

"Yes, Katherine," Mama said quietly. "Never quit a job halfway."

"We're not even halfway!" replied Katherine.

" *'The godly woman strengthens her arms,'* " Mama quoted. "We are not going to quit no matter how much our arms hurt.

"You will get over the tired arms. We'll enjoy the wallpaper for years!"

*   *   *

"Mama," Katherine observed, "look where the ceiling and the wall meet. We have jagged edges, don't we? And they don't always meet."

Mama nodded.

"It's almost impossible to cut wallpaper so that ceiling and wall meet perfectly. That would take expensive paper and better tools than we have."

"And these bumpy old walls make it harder, too, right?"

"Right again! How you notice things!"

Katherine was embarrassed. It wasn't often that Mama complimented her.

"Is there anything we can do about those jagged edges, Mama?"

Mama nodded, looking pleased.

"Yes, we bought narrow strips of wallpaper called *borders*. When we finish hanging the wallpaper, we will add a border along the top edge of the room. The border will cover the jagged edges to give the room a finished look."

"May I see the borders?" Katherine thought it fun to do something new.

Mama hesitated.

"Not now, Katherine. It will only waste time. We'll finish this last strip of ceiling, have lunch, do the wallpaper — and then I'll get out the borders. Right now they are on a shelf in the pantry closet."

That was answer enough. Wow! What a change!

Katherine was learning to be creative. To change ugliness to beauty.

*   *   *

· Lay ceiling paper on the floor . . .

· Spread paste over the paper . . . smoothly, smoothly . . .

· Hold it carefully while climbing onto the chair . . .

· Lift the thin, paste-heavy paper up, up, up to the ceiling . . .

· Rub it, rub it, rub it, rub it until smooth . . .

Over and over and over. Katherine's arms were so numb and sore!

. . . And that's when it happened.

*   *   *

Papa was starting to hang the ninth and last strip of ceiling paper.

Mama held up one end of the ceiling wallpaper with a wide broom.

Katherine stood on a chair between them, holding the paper as high as she could. It was heavy and wanted to fall down. She had to stretch her arms upward their full length to hold it against the ceiling.

How her arms ached! She could hardly hold them up anymore.

Spots were swirling in front of her eyes. She was getting *so tired* . . .

Climbing onto the chair holding the last strip of ceiling paper, suddenly she slipped. Before she could stop herself, her whole arm . . . oh, no!

Her hand and one whole arm had gone right through that wallpaper!

Katherine's eyes bulged out and her mouth hung open with horror.

Six-year-old Dorothy stood in the doorway watching. John Cecil had just fallen asleep, so she was ready to help with dinner.

"Katherine Kroontje! Look what you did!" exclaimed Dorothy.

Katherine's eyes were wide with horror. Had she ruined everything? She could only stare at her arm sticking right through that wallpaper. WHAT NOW?

*   *   *

Katherine expected Papa and Mama to scold her. After all, Mama wanted her walls beautiful. And she had ruined it.

So the last sound she expected was the sound she heard.

Papa was laughing!

Not a small chuckle. Not even a little laugh. Papa's laugh was a deep, deep, belly laugh. He exploded with laughter!

Mama usually didn't laugh so quickly at accidents. But when she heard Papa's belly laugh, she saw the humor and began to laugh as well.

Mama must have been tired, too, Katherine decided. She couldn't stop laughing once she began. She laughed until tears ran down her cheeks.

That made Dorothy start laughing, too.

All three of them pointed at Katherine and howled with laughter . . .

. . . While Katherine stood there, arm through the paper, eyes wide with horror. Having no idea what she should do next.

*   *   *

When Mama finally calmed down, she still kept chuckling.

"Oh my, Girl, if you could have seen yourself! If only I had a camera!"

"Well now, this strip of paper is ruined, eh?" chuckled Papa, swiping tears from his cheeks. "Let's start it over again.

"Good thing it's the last strip of ceiling. Good thing there's paper left."

And, while they cut another strip, laid it out, pasted it, hung it, and rubbed it smooth, Papa and Mama chuckled the entire time. They would calm down for a minute, glance at each other, and start laughing all over.

It surprised Katherine. Anything expensive was usually taken seriously. Nothing might be wasted. And they had wasted a whole strip of wallpaper!

But it also made her less embarrassed. At least they'd ended the morning with a laugh.

*   *   *

Laughter continued in the afternoon, as they pasted the half walls.

Walls were easier to do. Strips were shorter. Since they didn't have to concentrate so much, they talked while they worked.

The challenge with walls was to keep wallpaper panels vertical. The patterns had to fit carefully next to each other.

To make that happen, Mama tied yarn onto a heavy pencil. The hanging pencil pulled the yarn straight down. The yarn made a good guideline.

Now Papa did most of the hard work. Mama and Katherine spread paste onto the back of the short wallpaper strip. Katherine carried a strip to Papa. Papa put it up and smoothed it out while Katherine and Mama got the next strip ready.

Sometimes paste oozed out at the edges. Then it was Katherine's job to use a warm wash cloth to wipe the ooze away. For that, she'd stand on a chair right next to Papa, who was still rubbing the wallpaper smooth.

*   *   *

Yes, wallpapering was hard work. Very hard . . .

But what a change it made to the looks of the house!

Yes, the finished project was beautiful . . .

Katherine loved the pretty yellow sunflowers, the white daisies with their brown and yellow centers, the fluttering butterflies, and little bluebells. The wallpaper made the kitchen into a garden.

Yes, Mama was right . . .

It was worth the tired arms. Though all her muscles ached, Katherine felt like she was floating.

Because now the yellow house felt like home!

> "O my God, I trust in Thee . . .
> Let not mine enemies triumph over me."

Willie and Katherine with Uncle Bill home on furlough, 1942

Chapter 6: December 7, 1941

WAR!!

Sunday. December 7, 1941.
A day of rest. A day to worship God. To forget politics.

*   *   *

Katherine, sitting in church, remembered the conversation Papa had with the Tilstra uncles at the Memorial Day family reunion in May of 1940. Everyone on the porch that evening had discussed the possibility of war. They had thought that war had to happen. And the three youngest Tilstra uncles knew that they were the right age for being drafted as soldiers.

Uncle Bill hadn't waited for a declaration of war. He wanted to be ready. He joined 21 million young men who volunteered for service. Another 10 million men were later drafted.

Uncle Bill wanted to help the world get rid of that madman, Hitler.

And he hoped to help their Dutch relatives.

Both the Tilstras and the Kroontjes had relatives in the Netherlands. They were afraid of Nazi domination. It didn't matter to Hitler that the Netherlands was a "neutral" country. He wanted to rule over every country. He would use Dutch protection of the Jews as an excuse to rule them, too.

So Uncle Bill enlisted. He wanted to help in Europe to fight the Nazis and Hitler.

*   *   *

President Roosevelt was already drafting an army — getting ready for the possibility of war. Officially, the United States had not entered the war. President Roosevelt wanted the entire country united, agreeing that they must enter the war, before he took action.

What happened on December 7 was just what was needed.

No one had expected it.

There were people, later, who said it should have been expected. There were intelligence leaks that warned the government about it.

Despite that, it was unexpected. No one had believed the intelligence.

It shocked the entire nation.

It shocked the entire *world*.

*　　*　　*

Uncle Bill had enlisted in the navy less than a week before.

The whole family worried about Uncle Bill.

Before Uncle Bill enlisted, Papa and Mama visited the Tilstra farm once or twice per year. Starting with December 7, they visited as often as possible. They went to support Grandpa and Grandma — and to read letters from Uncle Bill. When Mama wrote letters, it might take a month to receive an answer.

*　　*　　*

"Gerrit, no snowballs!"

Katherine frowned at Gerrit. Ever the tease, he had made a snowball from the light dusting of snow on the ground.

Willie merely chuckled. "Anyway, Gerrit, don't *throw* snowballs unless they're totally snow. That's the rule, right?"

"Yes!" Dorothy chimed in indignantly. "You know what Papa said!"

"Okay, okay," Gerrit grinned, dropping his dirty snowball. "I won't throw it. But you have to admit, it will be fun when we have the first REAL snowfall."

It was Sunday afternoon. The family was home from church. After Sunday dinner, the children had gone back outdoors to check on the lightly falling snow.

Laughing and teasing, they continued to banter with each other. The brisk, late-fall or early-winter weather had them in a good mood.

Katherine returned to the house first. She hoped for a few hours of reading before evening chores.

But reading was forgotten when she entered the house.

It was forgotten the second she saw Papa standing behind Mama, stroking her hair. He was trying to comfort Mama, who was sobbing uncontrollably. In all their memories, this was only the second time the children saw Mama cry.

That moment changed the next four years.

*   *   *

"Mama, what's wrong?" exclaimed Katherine.

All four children entered the kitchen but stopped short inside the doorway. Katherine ran to Mama and knelt to look into her eyes.

Dorothy ran to Papa.

Papa answered them. Mama was too upset to talk.

"Children, we turned on the radio after you went outside. We learned that today — at 7:55 A.M. Hawaii time — Japan bombed Pearl Harbor. For us, that happened this morning, just as we were leaving church."

"Pearl Harbor?" echoed Willie. "Isn't that where Uncle Bill is stationed?"

"Yes," added Gerrit, who had been absorbing every detail about the war since Uncle Bill enlisted. "That's where President Roosevelt stationed most of our air force and navy, isn't it? Over by Hawaii in Pearl Harbor?"

Papa nodded, his face totally serious.

"You boys are correct," he responded. "That's what has upset Mama. Because just today, the war took a whole new course.

"So far the war has been in Europe. The United States is preparing for the possibility of fighting in Europe.

"But today, Japan entered the scene.

"Japan flew a whole fleet of airplanes into Pearl Harbor. 183 planes! They bombed our air force bases on land first. Every airplane is destroyed. Then, they bombed the ships in the harbor. Every major ship in the harbor was bombed!"

Everyone knew what he meant.

That meant Uncle Bill's ship had been bombed, too.

*   *   *

The whole family had followed reports of aggression. *Hitler* — of Germany — invaded Austria, Czechoslovakia and Poland. *Mussolini* — of Italy — invaded Ethiopia. *Franco* — of Spain — was fighting a rebel war and captured Madrid. *Tojo* — militant general under the meek Emperor Hirojito of Japan — bombed an American gunboat in China . . . but then Japan backed off, apologized, and paid two million dollars as an apology.

Katherine had heard President Roosevelt stress that America was a "Good Neighbor." That meant the United States was *not* aggressive. It would remain friendly no matter what neighboring countries were doing. The United States pulled out of Haiti and out of Cuba even though these close-by nations had anti-democratic turmoil.

Roosevelt had said: "I have seen war. I have seen war on land and sea. I have seen blood running from the wounded . . . I have seen the agony of mothers and wives. I hate war."

It was called an *isolationist* policy. It meant, "Leave the others alone."

The *isolationist policy* made Mama — and Katherine — hopeful that the United States would stay out of the war. They didn't want to see Uncle Bill fighting and maybe killed.

Papa was doubtful. How could the United States stay out of a war when Spain, Italy, Germany, and Russia — invading Finland — were all becoming aggressors? When Japan was building its military?

No one had seemed overly aware of the threat of Japan. True, American Ambassador Joseph Gates in Tokyo predicted that Japan would attack Pearl Harbor. But everyone thought he was an alarmist. He wasn't taken seriously.

Japan, that little country, attack the United States? Ridiculous!

Meanwhile, the world thought the United States was weak.

They thought the United States would let anything happen anywhere.

*   *   *

The United States' army and navy were ridiculously small. President Roosevelt knew that they had to be increased. He had said in a speech in Chicago that the totalitarian powers could get 1,500 aircraft into South America in one night . . . while "we have 80 planes that could get there in time to meet them."

When Hitler in 1940 began bombing Great Britain, Roosevelt felt he had to help. He loaned England 500,000 rifles and other arms. He gave them 50 old destroyers in exchange for leases on British bases in the Caribbean. In March of 1940, Congress voted to "lend" Britain 7 billion dollars worth of arms — more to come later. Helping Great Britain was almost as if the United States was already in the war, even though it officially wasn't.

Japan, meanwhile, kept doing aggressive things. It signed pacts with Hitler and with Franco. Roosevelt that summer had cut off U.S. oil to Japan. That was bad because Japan got 80% of its oil from the United States.

The United States had slapped Japan on the wrist. And Japan was in an ugly mood. It wouldn't take any kind of insult.

It moved its growing air force to Formosa — on ships. Ready to strike.

And now, it had struck. On Sunday morning, December 7, 1941. In Pearl Harbor, where Uncle Bill was stationed.

*   *   *

Katherine wouldn't learn details about Pearl Harbor until later.

Uncle Bill lived. It took a week to learn that.

He wrote a few things in letters. But he was not allowed to write important things. His letters were read and important things blacked out. And later, he was reluctant to talk about the war. His memories were too horrible.

Mostly, Katherine learned a little here and a little there.

Mostly, she learned things from the radio and newspapers.

What she learned little by little was that Uncle Bill was assigned to the *Arizona*, the first destroyed ship in Pearl Harbor. But he was not on the ship when it was torpedoed. He had arrived in Hawaii on Saturday, December 6, but never actually got on the ship. On Sunday, he had gone to church so was on land, planning to go to the *Arizona* later that day.

Coming out of church, Uncle Bill saw other ships attacked in the harbor. The *West Virginia* was on fire and sank. The *Oklahoma* was struck by five torpedoes and sank with its bottom pointing upwards toward the sky.

Survivors from ships found themselves in a harbor covered with gas and oil. Whenever they swallowed water, they gagged on gas and oil. All around floated debris from ships and dead bodies of fellow sailors.

Of the living sailors, many were wounded and groaning in pain.

Altogether, 18 ships were destroyed or badly disabled. 188 planes were destroyed and 159 more were damaged. More than 2,400 Americans were killed — half of them from the first and largest ship attacked, the *Arizona* — Uncle Bill's ship. Being in church had saved Uncle Bill's life.

*   *   *

If Japan had chosen another way to gain its ends — like invading Southeast Asia — it might have gotten what it wanted, mastery of China, without world war.

Instead, the bombing of Pearl Harbor united the United States.

President Roosevelt never slept the night of December 7th. Overnight, he made plans. He went to Congress in the morning. The Senate voted 82 to 0 to go to war. The House voted 388 to 1 for war. Only one representative in the whole United States voted against the war!

Three days later, Germany and Italy declared war on the United States.

The whole world was now at war. The United States was definitely in the war, too.

What would happen next? How would this war change their lives?

Sunday, December 21, 1941 (Christmas Letter)

Dear Uncle Bill,

To think that when you registered for the navy in Des Moines, you were sent straight to California and then put on a "potato boat" to go to Hawaii! I guess they know a good farm boy makes a good soldier, huh?

What a shock two weeks ago when Japan attacked Pearl Harbor! Since President Roosevelt practiced an "isolationist" policy, we hoped we wouldn't actually be in the war. Japan changed all that, though.

We were all thankful that you hadn't arrived at Pearl Harbor even a day or two earlier. Then you would have been aboard the Arizona when it was attacked. We see it as God's hand that led you to be in church on Sunday morning and so spared you the destruction of the ships in the harbor.

It must have still been hard, though, since you saw that horrible attack and now have to help clean up that mess. We all wonder what your next role in this war may be.

Not a lot has happened here at home in the month you've been gone — unless you want to hear about chickens squawking! Next time I write a letter, I'll let you know what new things are happening here.

May God continue to guard you every day while you serve Him in the navy. We pray for your life to be spared even though we know that to go to heaven is more glorious.

Your niece,
Katherine Kroontje

"Even a child is known by his doings, whether they be good or whether they be evil."

Midland #2 School in 1942. Gerrit is at left. Dorothy is below splotch

Chapter 7. April 13, 1942

Recess Shenanigans

Racism was not an issue in Iowa during World War II.

True, in much of the United States, there was an abundance of anti-German and anti-Japanese attitude. American Japanese were imprisoned in American concentration camps. No, there was no physical persecution; no one was shot or put in a gas chamber. But many lost their life savings and nearly starved. Children lost friends and years of schooling.

That wasn't true in Iowa. In Iowa, although intense anger was felt against both Germany and Japan, everyone understood that Americans were Americans. American Germans hated German imperialism. American Japanese hated Japanese imperialism.

*　　*　　*

When Katherine lived in her first home, the little white house, and attended Midland School #4, she was alone in her class. In Midland School #3, Katherine's school while she lived in the little yellow house, she had for one year only two classmates — both boys, both with the last name of Dirks. The Dirks were cousins but didn't look or act at all alike. Melvin Dirks was light-haired, a good student with good manners. John Dirks was dark-haired and a prankster.

Katherine got along okay with both of the Dirks.

In her second year at Midland #3, a new family attended the school. Their last name was Minerts. They lived the farthest of anyone from school, two miles to the north. There was no school in their district, so Midland #3 was the closest school. There were three Minerts: Lowell, a boy, the oldest; Lyla, a girl, the youngest, Dorothy's age; and Enola, a petite, brown-eyed girl, Katherine's age. Now Katherine had a girl in her grade.

Both the Dirks and the Minerts were of German ancestry.

Katherine, the only Dutch girl, was the minority in her eighth grade. In fact, all the students were of German descent . . . except for the Kroontje family.

*   *   *

Midland School #3 was larger and more upscale than Midland #4 had been. Although also a one-room school, it had student desks in three rows of five, enough for fifteen students. The desks all faced the teacher's desk and chalkboard at the front. Along the side were four large windows. The whole side of the room was windows. They allowed in lots of light.

Midland #3 had a finished basement under the school. The furnace and coal were in the basement. In cold weather, the teacher went to school early to shovel coal into the furnace and get the school warm. If the classroom became cold during the morning, the teacher would again stoke the furnace at noon. The children seldom shivered during school time.

On cold days, the children reached school with cold feet. They headed for the register of the furnace. It was in the center of the classroom, where heat from the furnace came through the floor.

Of course, the littlest children got to stand on the register first. Older children never tried to take away that privilege. But Enola and Katherine would stand as close as they could get to the register. As soon as the younger children moved off, they stood on the register, clapping hands and stamping feet.

Doing things like that together made the girls feel like friends. It was fun.

*   *   *

It took awhile for the boys of German ancestry to accept the Kroontjes of Dutch ancestry. Until they did, the Kroontje boys often stood alone at recess.

It didn't bother Katherine that Enola was German. The Germans fighting the war were across the ocean. This petite German girl in school was a nice girl. Katherine and Enola would help each other with assignments and play games together at recess.

Because they lived two miles apart, they never became friends who visited each others' homes. They were just in-school friends. Classmate friends. A dark-eyed German girl and a blue-eyed Dutch girl. Yes, they liked each other.

*   *   *

In one area, Katherine was different. Katherine was timid about breaking rules. Other girls obeyed rules in the classroom but enjoyed watching boys' pranks.

And boys, being boys, would every so often try out the teacher.

Usually, recesses were just fun. They would play any of several games. Five games Katherine remembers were:

1. *Baseball.* Both boys and girls would join in playing baseball to make the teams fair. In a small school, everyone had to cooperate.

2. *Red Rover.* The children would divide into two teams that were about equal for strength. Smaller children would hold hands with stronger children. The teams would take turns holding hands in a straight line and chant: "Red Rover, Red Rover, send _(name)_ right over!" Whichever person they chose from the other team had to run as fast as possible and try to break through the line at a weak spot. If he broke through, he could choose someone to come back and join his team. If he couldn't break through, he had to remain and become part of that team.

3. *Drop the Hanky* was too easy to play very often but little children loved it and so, for them, everyone occasionally played it. Everyone stood in a circle holding hands, while an "it" person walked around the outside. "It" would drop a hanky behind someone and then start running, trying to get around the circle and back to that person's spot before he caught up and tagged him out.

4. *Musical Chairs* was an indoor game for bad weather.

5. *Eeny-Einie-Over* was played over the school's coal shed. The children divided into teams, half on each side of the coal shed. Team 1 would throw a ball over the shed. Team 2 would catch the ball and then run to try to tag someone from the opposite team. The tagged person then had to join Team 2. Eeny-Einie-Over was a favorite game, chosen often.

The teacher seldom came outside for recess. She had to put all the assignments for the afternoon on the board. The children chose the games. The only time the teacher became involved was when there were problems.

*   *   *

Behind the school was a hill, perfect for sledding. In winter, the older boys took along sleds. It was too difficult for little children, and the girls didn't want to slide down.

What the boys liked to do was to stir up a little trouble. They would wait until the last minute of recess, just before the teacher rang the bell, and then head for the hill. It looked like they were innocently having fun when, in fact, they were trying to stall and make school late. Just as the teacher rang the bell, they would begin sliding down the hill, one at a time, taking turns. By the time they were all down the hill, they were late for class.

The first time this happened, Miss Eihausen just warned the boys. It must not happen again! When it happened again, she became very stern. She made all the boys stay in at recess and write lines promising not to do this again.

But it was such fun, they did it again. And again. And again.

Each time the teacher made them miss a recess, but they did it anyway.

They did it to tease the teacher. They thought they could get by with it.

*   *   *

It upset Katherine when Gerrit joined in. She knew that he did it to make friends with the German boys. But if Papa found out, Gerrit would have more discipline than just staying in at recess.

Today, April 13, was a cold day. Snow had fallen during the night. It was perfect for sledding. Gerrit had his sled along. Katherine knew his intention.

"Gerrit, don't you go sledding down that hill," she warned him.

One girl overheard Katherine. She looked at Katherine in surprise. "I'd rather be a dark-eyed German than a yellow-bellied Dutchman!" she told Katherine.

At the time, Katherine didn't understand the remark. Later, that remark made Katherine realize something: American Germans were sensitive about being German while European Germans were causing a world war.

After that, Katherine didn't dare scold Gerrit anymore.

What the boys forgot was that the school board was to meet that night. The school board met once a month and the teacher always had to report.

As soon as Gerrit realized that the school board met that night, he knew he was in trouble. Big trouble. Because Papa was on the school board.

No, Katherine hadn't said anything at home. Neither had Dorothy.

He had only himself to blame.

*   *   *

What actually happened? Did the teacher tell the school board? Did she mention Gerrit's name? Was Gerrit disciplined?

Well, I guess you'll have to ask Gerrit. Because Katherine doesn't remember. That was between Papa and Gerrit.

Or else, you can guess . . .

Because, whatever happened, after the school board meeting, the boys never pulled that prank again.

Chapter 8. August, 1942

Piano Lessons and Sprouting Potatoes

Nowadays, if people take piano lessons, they take them for years and years. They might start lessons in third grade and take them all the way through high school. Maybe all the way through college.

When Katherine took lessons, it was a major luxury. As a luxury, the money spent did not assist with daily expenses. As a luxury, it could last only as long as was absolutely necessary.

Katherine was thankful that her lessons lasted for one year.

*   *   *

The day Papa bought the piano, Katherine thought she would begin piano lessons immediately. She couldn't wait!

However, Papa procrastinated. So many things were going on right then. Mama had Baby John and needed time to gain strength. The house needed wallpapering. Having just moved onto the second farm, there were all sorts of farm things to get finished.

Katherine's lessons waited. The piano waited, too.

That didn't mean there was no music in the home in the meantime. Papa often pulled out his harmonica and played lively tunes on it. Later, Gerrit and John both played the harmonica as well. And Mama, though she played no instrument, loved to sing. She sang as she washed dishes, as she hung clothes on the line outside, as she took care of her red peonies around the house.

And the children sang along with Mama. They learned to harmonize, singing parts as they sang. It made work become fun.

The piano was simply one more form of delightful music.

*   *   *

Finally, in the fall of 1941, Papa found a piano teacher.

By then, Katherine was in her second-to-last year of school. That one year she took lessons, the year when she was eleven. Only one year — but what a precious year it was!

*   *   *

Katherine's teacher was Miss Williamson.

Miss Williamson was not a young teacher. She was a lady in her sixties. Quite a lady! In a day when few women learned to drive, she drove her own Model A Ford.

From the start, Katherine loved her. She would come to the house to teach lessons. She dressed like a school teacher, with a neat, dark skirt and a white blouse. Katherine had seen those kinds of clothes in the SEARS' catalogue and thought Miss Williamson probably bought them from the catalogue. Of course, she never asked such questions.

With such a neat teacher, it would be embarrassing to be in farm clothes with dirty face or hands. Katherine always dressed neatly, and didn't want to do chores before lessons because then she would be dirty.

Mama was also concerned that the house be clean when the teacher arrived. It would never do to have gossip around town that they were poor housekeepers! True, the teacher was too nice to gossip anyway . . . but Mama wasn't taking chances.

Miss Williamson didn't charge much for lessons. That was why Papa and Mama could afford them. Katherine could have three lessons for just $1.00. It was a bargain! But even bargains could be hard to pay for.

Katherine knew that her lessons meant sacrifice for her parents. It meant that Mama kept wearing the same dress to church even though the fabric was wearing thin. It meant that Papa wore the same old shoes which he had to patch over and over. He kept extra soles on hand and, when the old shoes got holes in the bottom, he used his gadget to nail on new soles.

Papa and Mama never said those things.

But Katherine could see. She knew they were letting her take lessons even though there were many things that other people would put first.

Papa and Mama wanted music for her. Music in the service of God.

*   *   *

Piano lessons were always on the same day of the week. Miss Williamson was always prompt. Exactly at 4:00, every Friday, she arrived for lessons.

Miss Williamson never told Katherine how fast to progress. She was very kind. She left the speed entirely up to Katherine.

Papa and Mama let Katherine practice as often as possible. She rushed through chores after school so she could practice a few minutes before supper. After supper she rushed through dishes so she could practice before baby John was put to bed. Every spare minute she was at the piano.

As a result, she progressed rapidly.

She also learned well because of Miss Williamson's method of teaching. She didn't simply ask Katherine to play songs and allow her to move on if they were poorly done. She expected Katherine to *memorize* the songs. Every song.

The series of books which Miss Williamson used was the *Schaum* Piano Lesson Books. These were combined with the *Thompson* Piano Lesson Books. John Thompson had been one of the first men to write piano lesson books for young students . . . but his series had progressed too fast. John Schaum had broken down these lessons into smaller steps. It was easier to learn that way.

Within a year, Katherine had gone through three levels of music books. They were called the Preparatory Level, the First Level, and the Second Level. She was partway through the Third Level. There were eight levels in all, but Katherine had to quit because Miss Williamson moved away.

For a short while, Katherine took lessons from another teacher . . . but then she, too, moved away. Then Katherine took lessons through the mail, with no teacher to evaluate her. She just practiced music she received.

Formal lessons lasted for only one year — in seventh grade, the year she was eleven, and through that summer, after she turned twelve.

*   *   *

In summer, it wasn't easy to be ready for the teacher.

In July, Katherine was busy most of the day helping with outside chores and helping in the house. At 3:00 in the afternoon, Mama called her into the cellar to help sprout potatoes.

"But, Mama, Miss Williamson is coming for my piano lesson," Katherine protested. "I'm going to get all dirty!"

"I'm sorry, Katherine, but I need help. Work quickly and try to stay clean," Mama replied. At that moment, she was too busy to worry about Miss Williamson.

So, dirty or not, Katherine and Mama sat in the cellar and sprouted potatoes. Dorothy was upstairs watching two-year-old John and Baby Marvin.

"Mama, why do they call this 'sprouting'?" questioned Katherine, her eyebrows drawn together. She felt like arguing.

"What do you mean?" asked Mama.

"Well, sprouts are roots of the potato growing on the potato," replied Katherine. "But the potato grows its own roots, right? We don't make it sprout!

"I think," she added, nodding her head for emphasis, "that we should call this DEsprouting! The potato sprouts ... and we DEsprout it. So there!"

Mama merely chuckled.

"Whatever you call it, Katherine, you'd better hurry if you want to be ready for your teacher," she replied. And Katherine did hurry.

They finished DEsprouting the potatoes at five minutes to four ...

Barely enough time for Katherine to wash her hands and be ready.

*   *   *

When eighth grade began, Katherine had to quit piano lessons. She was beginning to play easy church songs. Papa thought that she could now progress on her own if he ordered lessons through the mail.

Katherine missed having formal lessons but she kept practicing. She wanted to be able to play all the songs in the hymnal used in church. Each week she tried to learn two new songs, practicing them until she had them perfect.

Sometimes Papa would come in and watch her practice. That would fluster her. With Papa watching, she made mistakes she hadn't made when she was alone.

As she improved, Papa sang along with songs she was playing. Sometimes he played along with her on his harmonica. That made her make mistakes, too, at first. But it was also fun. It made her practice harder.

Finally she could play well enough that she didn't have to stop and play parts over. Papa played or sang just like he sang in church.

That was when playing the piano became fun!

*   *   *

It was April of 1943. May was Katherine's last month of schooling. That month she would go to Rock Rapids for final testing. If she passed, she would graduate from eighth grade. Graduation was the third week of May.

Katherine returned from school one afternoon in April to find the minister's car parked outside the house. Dorothy ran ahead to find out what was happening.

Katherine entered the kitchen quietly, planning to slip through and go upstairs. Papa and Mama were at the table having coffee with the minister.

But as she entered, Papa held up one hand to stop her.

"Katherine," Papa said, "the minister has a request for you. Would you set your books down on the landing and join us?"

Setting her books down, Katherine saw Dorothy sitting halfway up the stairs. Dorothy's eyes were large as she shrugged at Katherine. She whispered, "Tell me what this is all about, okay?"

Dorothy liked to know what was happening!

*   *   *

Katherine shyly sat on a chair next to Papa and Mama.

"Katherine," the minister said kindly, reaching to shake her hand, "I've been hearing good things about your piano playing. Miss Williamson told me already a year ago that you were progressing well. I know you couldn't continue lessons but you've kept on practicing. Your Papa says you play well enough that he can sing along with you."

Katherine was embarrassed.

"I like to play," she admitted, her eyes on the floor, "but it's still hard for me to play well enough for Papa to sing along."

The minister nodded.

"I can understand that," he responded. "But this is why I'm here. Right now, we need players for church. Four girls your age are taking lessons. We are asking each of you to take turns playing for church services. Do you think you could do this?"

Katherine's mouth hung open in surprise.

"Sir, I can't play *all* the songs in the hymnal!" she stammered. "I can play the easier songs but not the hard ones."

"I expected that," the minister nodded. "But we have a real need.

"Here's my idea. The Sunday before you play, I'll choose songs that you can practice that week. I won't choose any songs that you think are impossible. If we do it that way, will you help us out?"

It scared Katherine but also made her feel proud.

"I tell you what," the minister continued, "at first you can play for one service, in the evening on Sunday. Once you feel more confident, you can play at both services. Even once a month would be a great help."

Katherine could tell that this made Papa happy. His eyes sparkled as he waited for her answer.

"I . . . I'll try, Reverend," she whispered.

"That's all we ask," the minister replied, standing. He reached again to shake her hand. "God bless you, my dear. I'm sure you will do a fine job.

"Do you think you can begin playing in May?"

Katherine was too shocked to answer.

But as the minister walked out to his car, she found herself in Papa's arms. His hug told her all she needed to know. He was proud of her.

For his sake, she would play her best.

For his sake, for Mama's sake, and for God's sake.

She owed her love of music to all three of them.

Sunday, December 13, 1942
(Christmas Letter)

Dear Uncle Bill,

One month after we joined the war, our teacher assigned us to make a scrapbook of the war. I am collecting every newspaper article I find. I will keep it up until the war ends . . . because you are in the war.

Papa talked about World War I the other day. He was a cook in the army in World War I, before he came to America.

When you joined the war, you thought you'd be crossing the Atlantic to fight Germany, as Pa did. Instead, you are crossing the Pacific to fight the Japanese. Who would have thought?

Just think of all that you've had happen in one year. Wow! First you spent half a year cleaning up the gruesome harbor mess. In June you spent two weeks on the USS Yorktown, which was supposed to take you to your own ship in the South Pacific, the USS Blue. But the Japanese really wanted the Yorktown and they got it, right while you were aboard.

You floated in the Pacific Ocean for 24 hours until an Australian ship picked you up and brought you to your own ship, the USS Blue. At last!

Yes, at last — after four months of trying to get there — you were on your ship. But only two months later, in August, the USS Blue was torpedoed and sank — with your life amazingly spared a third time.

And then God rescued you from the islands by the ship on which were the Millinex brothers. Another act of mercy! How wonderful that God used you to weld that ship and perhaps save the lives of your friends!

And now you are on the USS Patterson — a ship always in the thick of the fighting. We pray that God will continue to guard and protect you.

Major news at home this year was the birth of Marvin on May 4. He's already seven months old. He coos a lot; we all love both John and him. John is now walking all over and loves to climb! I can't wait until you can see them.

Praying for you daily,
Katherine Kroontje

PART II: 1943 – 1945

Fulltime at Home

. . .

and

. . .

War Effort

"Study to show thyself approved unto God . . ."

Midland #3 School in 1944. Left to Right: Nina Mae Buss, Phyl Eihausen, Dorothy Kroontje, John Kroontje, Marvin Kroontje, Marilyn Dieken, George Sharron, Don Dieken, Paul Buss, Gerrit Kroontje, Don Hoogland

Chapter 9. May, 1943

Graduation!

Two new dresses?

Katherine stared dreamily at the dresses hanging in her closet. She could hardly believe that Mama had given her *two* new dresses.

New? Well, one was hardly new. The dress was made-over from Mama's church maternity dress. It was a "peachy peach" colored print. Mama had taken her loose-fitting dress and made it into a form-fitting dress in a Princess style. It had an attractive, white lace collar.

"A dress for my Princess," Papa teased her. But he looked proud.

This dress was made for Katherine's testing-out day.

In order to graduate from eighth grade, Katherine had to go to the Rock Rapids' Public High School to be tested. All eighth graders from Lyon County, Iowa, had to be tested there. The testing was done the third week of May.

Everyone who passed the tests had to be there again the following week for graduation. Testing and graduation were both in the afternoon.

The second dress was for graduation. Katherine hugged herself, thinking how wonderful it would be to wear that store-bought dress.

She wouldn't think too much about it yet. First she had to pass the tests!

*   *   *

The Rock Rapids' Public High School was a huge building in the eyes of a girl who had only attended one-room schools. It was on a side street in the south part of Rock Rapids. Katherine had never before entered the building.

Katherine felt really fine in the dress made from Mama's maternity dress. It was just as nice as any other dress in the room. "Thank you, Mama," she whispered, even though Mama wasn't there to hear her.

Katherine couldn't believe all the students there. She should have figured out that there would be lots of them, since they came from all the grade schools in the county. Most of the grade schools were small like Katherine's. Only the grade school in Rock Rapids was larger.

All the students were quiet and respectful.

Testing had to be done in front of several authorized testers. Before they were tested, everyone sat on chairs in a large hallway. They were given instructions: be totally silent during the testing; anyone caught cheating was disqualified; only use lead pencils . . .

It was scary but, since Katherine wanted her graduation diploma, she breathed hard and listened carefully. Papa and Mama depended on her.

*   *   *

The standardized, written testing took between two to three hours.

They were tested on all areas of learning: spelling, comprehension, grammar, writing ability, math computation, math understanding, geography, science, and more.

Each test was timed. Most of them took twenty to twenty-five minutes. Students could not pick up their pencils until the starting time was announced, and had to lay down their pencils as soon as the time was over.

Although the tests covered lots of material, Katherine didn't find any of it too hard. Some tests she couldn't quite finish, though, and that bothered her.

It was a great relief when the clock said 4:00 and the tests were finished.

*   *   *

"Katherine . . ."

Katherine turned in surprise at the voice. Jessie was here?

"Jessie? Didn't you graduate last year?"

Jessie Smidstra had been Katherine's special friend in school when she lived in the Little White House. But they went to different schools and seldom saw each other since Katherine moved to the Little Yellow House.

"Oh, didn't you know? A county tester put our whole class back a year. Now I'm at the same level you are."

"Really?" exclaimed Katherine. "That's too bad, since you were always a good student. But how nice that we now graduate together! Assuming, of course, that we both pass the tests . . ."

Jessie looked thoughtful. "I didn't find the tests that difficult, did you?"

"No," agreed Katherine. "I was really worried when I came, but I thought I understood what I did. I hardly ever finished a test, though."

"Oh, neither did I!" exclaimed Jessie. "We weren't expected to, right? At least, that's what they said when we started."

"Yes, that's what I understood, too. They said some of the questions were at college level. So I hope it didn't matter."

"I'm sure we'll both pass," Jessie assured Katherine, then gave her an impulsive hug. "Oh! I'm glad we graduate together! Perhaps our parents can sit together next week. It feels great to have a friend in this crowd."

*　　*　　*

Papa was waiting for Katherine by the exit doorway.

"How'd it go, Princess?" he asked, ruffling Katherine's hair.

"Pa!" exclaimed Katherine, embarrassed. Then she answered his question. "I was awfully scared, Pa, but the testers were nice. I think I did okay.

"And guess what," she added with enthusiasm, "Jessie was there! We get to graduate together! Can you sit with Jessie's parents for the ceremony?"

"Whoa, Girl," Papa responded. "Before we make any plans, let's make sure you graduate, eh?" Then, seeing how crestfallen Katherine looked, he tweaked her ear and said, "Of course you'll graduate. We know you'll pass the tests. And, yes, we'll sit with the Smidstras."

"Oh, Pa," Katherine shook her head, "will you ever quit teasing me?"

"Nope," Papa responded, "and I hope you never quit enjoying it, either!"

*　　*　　*

A week later found Katherine back at the Rock Rapids' Public High School for the Lyon County Eighth Grade Graduation ceremony. She held tightly to Mama's hand, following her proud Papa.

Katherine didn't feel proud. She felt small and scared.

What was she doing here, a small-school student in this huge building?

The new dress Mama had bought her helped. She felt she was dressed as nicely as the other girls. The dress had been bought in the new JCPenney's store in Rock Rapids. She had been able to try it on right there to make sure it fit right. It was the prettiest dress she had ever owned. What Katherine didn't know was that the dress would disintegrate the first time she washed it!

The dress was a soft pink color. It had a layer of lace over the entire dress. It was made of a crepe material, different from the practical materials Katherine usually had. It had a pink belt and lacy white collar. Its short, angel-capped sleeves were just right for a warm day in May.

Papa looked over the crowd for the Smidstras. Not seeing them, he and Mama decided to sit down without them. Just then Katherine felt someone tickle her from behind. Squealing, she saw that Jessie had sneaked up on her. Her parents had parked the car and were at the same moment entering the doorway.

The two girls studied the large hallway while their parents walked to a row about halfway up. In front was a large raised platform with chairs for people who led the ceremony. Front row seats were reserved for graduates and teachers.

To the left in the front, a skilled musician was playing a sonata by Beethoven. Katherine could not yet play Beethoven but figured she would keep trying . . . and, maybe, someday she would!

The graduates were guided to a large room at the rear. The Superintendent of Lyon County High Schools, a stylishly dressed, stately lady, told them that they must line up in order according to their schools. She called off the schools' names until everyone was in line.

Jessie and Katherine couldn't sit together for the ceremony. Although they had begun school together, Katherine graduated from a different school.

Now it was 2:00. Time for the ceremony to begin.

*   *   *

The talented pianist in front began playing a graduation processional. The program called it *Pomp and Circumstance*. It was easy to walk in to that song.

The four adults who would sit on the platform led the processional. One of them was the Superintendent of the Lyon County High Schools. The three others were important teachers or leaders in the schools.

Although nervous, as Katherine passed Jessie, she gave her a timid smile. Jessie didn't seem nervous at all and smiled broadly back. Katherine was in the second row to the front. Jessie was behind her, just a few seats to her left. They couldn't look at each other during the ceremony.

After everyone was in their rows, the lady superintendent gave a signal and they all sat down together. There wasn't a sound in the large hall.

The lady speaker introduced herself and the other three people on the platform. She gave a ten minute talk about the importance of education and how proud parents were of their children who achieved this landmark. She pointed to the teachers and said how grateful she was that people would dedicate their lives to educating young people. Then she introduced the next speaker.

One by one, the three educators stood and gave short speeches. Some were five minutes, some were ten. Altogether, the speeches took twenty minutes.

"The program must be nearly finished," Katherine thought. And then the superintendent again stood up by the podium.

*   *   *

"Before we give out diplomas, there are some students who have done exceptionally well in some area of education," the superintendent said. "We would like to hand out certificates of award to those students. The certificates will be handed out, like the diplomas, in alphabetical order."

Katherine hadn't been told that there would be awards. But she didn't expect an award, anyway. After all, she hadn't played in sports or any form of competition. What award could she expect?

"John Ankers. Please come forward and receive an award for your fine essay in physics," the superintendent said. An obviously surprised young man went to the front and was given a rolled-up piece of paper, tied with a ribbon, from one of the educators. The other educators all solemnly shook his hand.

"Norma Coopers . . ." A second award, for being good in art.

"Cynthia Erdman . . ." A third award, for an outstanding poem.

"Paul Hookman . . ." Another award, for a clever science project.

"Katherine Kroontje . . ." WHAT? Had she heard right? Katherine's feet felt glued to the floor. She just stood there — until Jessie reached from behind and gave her a little push. Then she took a deep breath and walked as regally as she could to the front. She felt her heart pounding with every step.

"Katherine, you are given this award in recognition of your outstanding work in singing and piano playing. Congratulations!" said the superintendent, as she shook Katherine's hand. The next educator handed her a rolled-up award and also shook her hand. Then the other two educators shook her hand.

Katherine knew her face had turned red as she walked carefully back to her seat. She peeked at Jessie as she entered her row and saw a huge smile on her face. That comforted Katherine as she sedately sat down.

*　　*　　*

Several more awards were given out. Then it was time for diplomas.

One row at a time, students walked to the bottom of the stairs by the platform. As their names were called, one by one they marched across the platform, received their diplomas, shook the hands of the three educators and the superintendent, then walked down and back to their seats.

Katherine still felt hot from receiving the award, which she clutched in one hand. Now she blushed even more as she walked in front of everyone to receive her diploma.

By the time Jessie and everyone else received their diplomas, the ceremony had taken nearly two hours. Graduations were impressive!

*　　*　　*

Standing in the back after the recessional, Katherine was met by Jessie. Jessie was not shy and gave her another hug.

"Congratulations, Katherine!" she whispered. "You deserved that music award. You always loved singing, from the time you first came to school with your *Little Red Book*. Remember that first day of school?"

That made Katherine giggle. She felt some of her tenseness vanish. She had been so proud of that *Red Book*! She intended to keep it always. She would sing those songs as she worked in the fields or washed laundry in the summer kitchen. O yes, she loved music! That she had learned from Papa and Mama.

"I wish you had gotten an award, too, Jessie," she said sincerely. "You always did your best, too. They should have given you an award for being the best friend anyone could ever have!"

*   *   *

Parents pushed their way to the back, finding their students. Papa, just reaching them, overheard Katherine's remark to Jessie.

"Yes, Jessie, that would have been a deserved award," Papa said kindly. "It meant so much to us that you were Katherine's friend when she began school."

"Thanks, Mr. and Mrs. Kroontje. And thanks, Katherine!" Tears shone in Jessie's eyes as she gave Katherine a parting hug.

Graduation was over. It was time to go home, to a life without school.

Time to return to work on the farm . . . and whatever the future held.

"The Spirit also helpeth our infirmities:
for we know not what we should pray for as we ought."

Papa and Mama Kroontje ready for church, 1947

Chapter 10. October, 1943

How God Supplied Tires

One hand worrying his hair, Papa knelt and rubbed the farm wagon's tires.

Katherine and Gerrit, watching Papa, understood the problem. Next month would be oat harvesting. How was this to be done if the tires of the wagon were bald? If rationing made it impossible to get new tires?

*   *   *

It wasn't hard to remember when rationing began. Marvin Walter Kroontje was born on the morning of May 4, 1942. Papa had to go in for his first book of sugar rationing coupons on that same afternoon.

That's when rationing began on sugar and coffee. On Marvin's birth day.

Papa chuckled at the memory. He had to report the number of children in the family and said he had six.

The man issuing the stamps raised his eyebrows, because he knew Papa.

"Six?" he asked. "Last I knew, it was five!"

Papa explained that Marvin had just been born — and so received extra sugar stamps. The whole family was glad Marvin had been born that day!

*   *   *

Sugar rationing — and all kinds of other rationing — were a part of "war effort." The world war made it hard to get enough. Things first had to be sent to the soldiers. Everyone at home became involved in the "war effort."

The war effort took several forms.

One form of the war effort was that women, who used to stay at home, went to work doing things men normally did. They worked in factories producing war equipment. After the war many women continued to work away from home.

Mama didn't do that. But, like other women, she raised a "victory garden" of vegetables to feed themselves so canned food could go to the men at war.

Factories that had produced cars produced war machinery instead. So beginning in 1942, no more cars were produced until the war ended. Papa was thankful that he had bought a new car, a Ford Deluxe, in 1941. Since he bought a new car every ten years, this car would last until 1951.

Gasoline was rationed. A car was allowed four gallons of gasoline per week. Since that was the least any vehicle was allowed, the government called this "A" rationing. When Papa went to get gas, he handed the pump attendant — a woman — coupons from his "A" rationing book along with cash for the gas.

The maximum driving speed became 35mph to economize on gas. Even cartoon characters were used to promote this. Daffy Duck's cartoon shouted, "Keep it under 40!". Bugs Bunny had an "A" sticker on his airplane windshield which explained why his airplane plunged downward, out of fuel.

*   *   *

Children became involved in the war effort, too.

The minute the war began, the government knew it needed money to pay for the war. An important way it raised money was through "war bonds." Gerrit and Dorothy were encouraged to take to school at least a dime per day. With these dimes they bought little stickers to paste into war bond books. When a book was full with 187 stamps, they added another nickle and brought it to the post office. The post office gave them a "bond" worth $25 after the war ended.

If they saved enough for three or four bonds, they received a "Liberty Loan Pin" that they could proudly wear showing they had bought that many bonds. That was a goal towards which they worked.

Gerrit and Dorothy weren't just *given* these dimes. They had to *earn* them. They did extra work beyond normal chores. It made them feel *involved*.

Another way Gerrit and Dorothy helped was that they collected milk weed pods. To this author, milk weed pods are an annoyance: I think milk weed is pretty but hate it when the pods go to seed and produce "fluff" to blow all over. Gerrit and Dorothy loved the fluff. They gathered it from railroad tracks and ditches, stuffed it into bags, and brought it to school. It was made into parachutes for men on airplanes and insulation in jackets. That fluff saved many lives!

*   *   *

Papa understood rationing. It kept things fair.

Mama understood rationing, too. She always had a huge garden and was willing to make it larger to help the war. So there wasn't much sugar? Mama was creative. She got honey from an uncle . . . or bought "rock candy" in a huge box from the store. Rock candy was used in coffee in place of sugar.

Mama had always sold heavy cream and received butter in exchange. Now she switched to oleo-margarine. She stirred yellow into the white so it would look more like butter.

The family never drank alcohol — except at oat harvesting. Then harvesters expected a beer, since it helped offset the heat. Mama made her own home-brewed beer — which tasted better than store beer. One harvester asked her if he could buy his beer from her!

Yes, family members were all involved in war effort. They were glad to help. It made them feel as if they were, in these small ways, helping Uncle Bill.

*   *   *

Meanwhile, the family was eager for news from Uncle Bill. Since letters were monitored by the navy — confidential information blacked out with a marker — they often learned information long after it happened.

During the war, Uncle Bill was officially assigned to only three ships: the *USS Arizona*, the *USS Blue*, and the *USS Patterson*. However, he was aboard several ships, some for transport and some for rescue. Of these, the most significant ones were the *USS Yorktown* and the *USS Helm*. If you can remember these five names, you'll remember his story.

SHIP 1. On December 6 of 1941, Uncle Bill arrived at Pearl Harbor. His assigned ship, the *Arizona*, was the first ship torpedoed by the Japanese on December 7. Although half of his shipmates died, Uncle Bill was spared because he was on land at church. He never set foot on the *Arizona*.

SHIP 2. Uncle Bill spent nearly half a year helping clean up the harbor mess. He was assigned to the *USS Blue* by March but didn't reach it until the end of June. The *USS Yorktown* — a large aircraft carrier — was to transport him to the *Blue,* but he didn't get on the *Yorktown* until June.

Japan really wanted to destroy that ship, kept making up false reports that it had gotten it. Finally it did destroy it, in battles near Guadalcanal while Uncle Bill was still on it, being transported.

The *Yorktown* was the first of three ships sunk with Uncle Bill aboard.

SHIP 3. Uncle Bill was then picked up and transported by the (Australian) *HRMS Cambarria* to the *USS Blue* — finally reaching his assigned ship. In late August, however, only two months after he got aboard, this ship was attacked. The whole family remembers this story.

Uncle Bill was called onto the *USS Blue's* deck by a loudspeaker message. He had hardly arrived on deck when a Japanese torpedo struck the side of the ship by the boiler room. His buddies in the boiler room were scalded to death.

To escape the sinking ship, Uncle Bill had to jump from the deck into a small boat with interlaced wooden slats. The men sat with their feet in the water. The jump dislocated his ankle, which swelled and was very painful during his twenty-four hours in the water.

The *USS Blue* was the second ship sunk while Uncle Bill was aboard.

The family marveled when it learned this story because God had so clearly spared Uncle Bill's life a third time. It made them more serious in prayer.

SHIP 4. Uncle Bill was rescued from nearby islands by the *USS Helm*, on which were Howard and Robert Millinix, neighbor boys from back home. This was such a coincidence that the papers back home all picked up on it. They reported, "It's a small world after all!"

A doctor on this ship fixed Uncle Bill's dislocated ankle.

SHIP 5 — last ship. Now Uncle Bill was assigned to the *USS Patterson*. He was aboard this ship only a short time when the *Helm* — the ship *of* his friends — was torpedoed. The *Patterson's* loudspeaker asked for volunteer welders to help the nearby *Helm*. Since Uncle Bill was a welder, he volunteered to go down into the water to weld his friends' ship. Doing the job under-water was difficult — especially with his leg still in a cast — but it was enough to get the ship back to land for better repairs.

The *Helm* was not Uncle Bill's ship, however. After ten days on the *Helm*, the *Patterson* was back in port and picked him up again. Back on the *Patterson,* Uncle Bill served in this ship for nearly a year.

In November of 1943, a "Kamikaze," or Japanese suicide bomber, attacked the *Patterson.* That meant that a Japanese airplane dove straight into the ship, knowing the men on the plane would all be killed — but they were willing to die to destroy an important American ship.

When the suicide plane hit the ship, Uncle Bill was working in the engine department, as he did on every ship. Shrapnel from the attack severely injured him. He had shrapnel in his hands, his kidneys, and all over his body.

Because of the Japanese plane attack, the *Patterson* lost control and ran into another ship. The *Patterson* wasn't destroyed, only damaged. The entire front bow of the ship was severed, putting it out of commission until repaired.

This was the third ship disabled while Uncle Bill was on it.

His severe injuries ended the war for Uncle Bill. He had emergency medical help right away in Australia and in January was sent back to America for surgery in a naval hospital in Virginia. Altogether he was in war zones for two years and in medical treatment for over another year.

*   *   *

Now we go back to what was happening at home in Iowa.

Rationing became a problem for Papa when his farm wagon tires had worn out and he couldn't get new ones. Rubber was needed in the war.

Papa had done everything he could to stretch the life of his tires. He put his best tires on the car for church, put old ones on the wagons. He made trips to town only when it was really necessary. Neighbors bought things for each other to save on gas and tires. But Papa worried because his wagon tires were so threadbare that he wouldn't make it through oat harvest.

Well, he would do the best he could! If the tires gave out, he would take the tires off the car. But then, how would he get to church?

*   *   *

Meanwhile, for now Papa had to forget the war effort. He was an elder in the Rock Rapids Reformed Church, and it was his turn to go to Classis.

Classis in October of 1943 was held in a large hotel in Buckhill Falls, Pennsylvania. The entire delegation of men — elders and ministers from all the area Reformed churches — rode on a train to Pennsylvania. They couldn't take cars because of rationing. It was fun to all ride together and visit on the train.

Pennsylvania was a beautiful state. It had rolling hills, uncounted acres of lush green trees, and small rivers and lakes. Autumn scenery was breathtaking.

And outside of the meetings, in which church business took place, visiting over meals and coffee breaks was enjoyable. Papa loved being at Classis.

*   *   *

A major topic of conversation over coffee breaks was the war effort. Rationing and shortages were talked about frequently.

One coffee break, Papa visited with a minister from New Jersey.

"Mr. Kroontje, how is the war effort affecting you as a farmer?" the minister asked. He seemed genuinely concerned.

"Well," Papa responded, "in some ways it's easier for us than for folks in the city. We have enough meat since we butcher our own animals. We have ample gardens for fresh and canned produce.

"But my problem is tires. I stood and stared at my bald wagon tires a few days ago, wondering how on earth I would get harvesting done next month. I have to admit, it's hard not to worry when a problem like that is staring me in the face and I have no idea how to solve it!"

"Tires are your problem?" the minister responded. "You know, they don't limit tires for professional people. I can get any amount of tires I need. How about if I ship you tires?"

Papa was so surprised he nearly stuttered his thanks.

He wasn't sure if he could take the minister seriously.

*   *   *

But the minister was serious and dependable. A few weeks later, only days before oat harvesting was to begin, tires were shipped to their home. They were sent via regular postal service, so a mailman had to deliver them.

"Knock, knock!"

Papa was startled when the knock came during his morning coffee break. (Of course, he wasn't drinking real coffee but a coffee substitute.

Real coffee was for soldiers.) It wasn't too often that Papa's coffee break was interrupted. But he rose quickly to open the door.

The mailman had a huge smile on his face.

"Mr. Kroontje," he said, "I have a delivery for you that I didn't dare leave by the mailbox. I feel sure that if I left it there you would never see it. Can you help me bring it from the car?"

To Papa's astonishment, the mailman had a set of tires! Papa had almost forgotten the minister's words, thinking it was only conversation, not a real promise. But there, on the back seat, were those beautiful, brand new tires!

Papa could hardly believe it. Once again, God had provided his needs.

*   *   *

Of course, those new tires didn't go on the wagon. The wagon got the tires off the car, which was only a year old.

Now the family didn't have to worry anymore about a flat tire on their way to church. Instead, at church, they had a good story to tell. A story that glorified God — who hears prayer and supplies the needs of His children . . .

The needs of those at home as well as those fighting the war.

Chapter 11. November, 1943

The Electric Perm

Katherine squinted into the small, cloudy mirror on her wall.

The mirror was too opaque for a clear view of herself. She could see herself but not well enough to know whether she was good looking or plain. She could see a resemblance to the rest of the family.

But what Katherine was studying was not her face. She was studying her hair. She was comparing her hair with the hair of friends at church.

These friends had been to a new "beauty parlor" in Rock Rapids. The parlor had electricity . . . and could use electricity to make people beautiful.

What a wonderful thing electricity was! Katherine could only dream of its wonders: of flicking a switch, and making the house alive with light! Of having a furnace that didn't demand corn cobs, or coal, or any other dirty element! Of plugging in a toaster for bread! She had heard of those things but they were for city people, for rich people, not for country folks like the Kroontjes.

And now there was an electric-powered beauty parlor in town.

Would it be possible . . . ?

*　　　*　　　*

Mama had her own method for fixing the girls' hair. She used rags.

Mama would cut an old muslin rag into strips twice as long as the hair she planned to work with. Her goal was pipe curls.

Mama would wet the muslin strip. Then she would separate Katherine's hair into small strips all the way around her head. She would take a swathe of hair and wrap it around the muslin to make a curl. Mama folded the extra length of muslin up to the top of the pipe curl and tied a knot so the curl couldn't unfold.

Katherine would have to protect those pipe curls while her hair dried.

Once her hair was dry, she could undo the pipe curls herself, shake her hair out a bit, and she was pretty enough to go anywhere.

For school pictures, church, or a program, she might add a flower or a bow.

Mama had been curling Katherine's hair that way for the last four years.

*   *   *

Katherine had to giggle at one memory.

When Katherine was twelve years old, Mama had set her hair one afternoon in preparation for a program that evening.

Then Papa offered to take Mama on a quick drive to town.

That didn't happen often. Usually Papa did errands, following a list Mama made. She only went to town for special things.

Katherine doesn't remember why Mama went to town that day. To pick up a bow for the evening program? To make her daughter extra pretty?

Mama left so quickly she didn't take time to empty the dishpan.

As soon as she left, Gerrit saw the dishpan with water in it. Being a typical boy, he invented a game.

"Let's see who can dunk his head in the water the longest," he challenged.

Willie thought Gerrit was silly but he played along anyway, just for fun.

Gerrit went first. He dunked his head under the water for about fifteen seconds. Then he came up, sputtering and coughing.

"Your turn, Willie!"

Willie took a deep breath and was able to stay under the water much longer. Maybe even half a minute.

Willie's face was red but triumphant when he emerged from the water.

"I won!" he crowed.

"Your turn, Katherine," challenged Gerrit.

"But my curls . . ." responded Katherine. She hated to refuse a challenge!

"Ho, who cares about curls?" scoffed Gerrit. "Besides, you don't have to dunk so far they get ruined. Just get your face under water, that's all."

The water was clear water, not full of soapsuds.

The challenge was too much to resist.

Katherine dunked. She lasted twenty seconds — more than Gerrit, less than Willie.

But her hair had also fallen into the water. It was soaking wet.

And some of the muslin had come loose. Katherine tried to tie it back up but she wasn't good at it like Mama. Besides, there wasn't time for it to dry again.

Mama came home about fifteen minutes later.

*   *   *

My, Mama was upset! Her eyes flashed at Katherine.

Then, shrugging her shoulders, Mama sighed, "Well, it is your own fault. You will simply have to wear your hair in pigtails tonight. You have no choice."

While Katherine's lips trembled, Mama undid the muslin strips and combed the hair back out. Mama pulled the hair into pigtails. She added a bow to each pigtail. There was just enough curl left where the hair hadn't gotten wet to make it look a little special — just not as special as pipe curls.

Katherine had been devastated. Her special evening had been ruined.

But . . . yes, she knew it was her own fault.

*   *   *

Now, Katherine was a whole year older. She was thirteen.

Thirteen was grown-up! So much older than twelve!

Looking at her hair in the cloudy mirror, she compared her hair with Dorothy's. Dorothy's hair was naturally straight. It also looked nice but had to be trimmed regularly because it had no curl of its own.

Katherine's hair had a bit of natural curl. Just enough to keep it wavy.

However, it didn't have curls all the time.

Girls whose hair was curled at the beauty parlor had curls all the time! That's what the large poster on the parlor window promised. Curls that lasted. All day long and all month long. One sentence especially caught everyone's eyes: *Be beautiful all the time!*

The thought was dreamy. How wonderful, to be beautiful all the time!

*   *   *

Mama had seen the beauty parlor ads, too. And she had overheard people talking about it.

When Katherine asked her if she could get an electric perm, Mama didn't refuse. She said she would talk it over with Papa and let her know.

Katherine was delighted when Mama said that Papa had given permission.

Papa had to take her to Rock Rapids for the perm. Before he dropped her off, he gave Katherine enough money for the perm and an ice cream cone afterwards. He said to her, "You are now a teenager. You're already in Young People's Bible Study. Make yourself pretty for that, okay?"

He gave a little wink and waved as he walked to the grocery store.

*   *   *

Katherine felt awed to be walking into a modern hair parlor all by herself.

She looked around the room and felt even more awed.

The parlor had fancy chairs that could swivel. My! They must be expensive!

Hanging from the ceiling, above the swivel chairs, were the strangest contraptions she had ever seen. An electric wire connected to a long tube which branched out into several smaller tubes. The branching tubes ended with curling clamps. What were these strange things?

A pretty girl with curls all around her face walked up to Katherine. Katherine couldn't take her eyes off the girl's gorgeous curls.

"Oh, could I possibly look like that?" she whispered.

*   *   *

Within minutes, Katherine was seated in one of those swivel chairs.

Within several minutes more, the girl with the beautiful curls had curled Katherine's shoulder-length hair inside curlers and had attached the curlers into those tubes hanging from the ceiling.

That was when the day-dreaming ended.

That was when the horror began.

*   *   *

What that contraption hanging from the ceiling did was curl your hair. The electricity caused heat and heat did the curling.

It was HOT! Katherine later learned that some people had the hair burned off their heads. Some people actually burned their heads.

It was a horrible machine! Once your hair was in it, you couldn't get free.

The machine stayed hot for several minutes, as long as the lady with the beautiful curls thought was necessary. Then she released the machine and freed Katherine.

*　　*　　*

Katherine watched the beautiful girl undo her curlers. One by one.

She watched as the girl reached for a brush and began brushing.

Looking into a large mirror in front of the swivel chair, she waited for the beauty to unfold. The promised beauty. The beauty that lasted all the time.

Instead, what she saw was as horrible as the curling contraption. Her hair was frizz! Solid frizz! Not a curl in it, just frizz!

*　　*　　*

When Papa returned for his beautiful daughter, he found her sitting on a bench in front of the beauty salon, sobbing. At first, he didn't even recognize her.

When he did, he at least had the sense not to laugh. He seemed to understand that she had wanted to be beautiful. That she had been made unrecognizable instead. And that this wasn't a time to laugh.

Papa simply put his arms around Katherine and gave her a hug. Tilting her chin upwards, Papa said kindly, "It'll grow out."

Katherine nodded. Yes, it would grow out.

But *why* had it turned out so awful? *Why* hadn't she looked like the girl with gorgeous curls?

Katherine had no desire to get that ice cream cone.

*　　*　　*

There was nothing to do except look frizzy for a month while the hair grew out. Katherine felt like an ugly duckling. She tried to stay out of sight.

Eventually, Katherine's hair returned to normal. Mama curled it again.

Three months later, Mama gave Katherine her first home perm. It was much like home perms still are today. (1) Pour on solution. (2) Roll hair with tiny curlers. (3) Rinse. Pour on another solution. (4) Rinse and dry.

Mama did everything this time — and several more times. It turned out well. Katherine's hair stayed curly all the time.

But Katherine never forgot the day she had the electric hair perm . . . or the month afterwards, when her hair was *frizzy* all the time.

Modernization did not always mean improvement!

Christmas Letter 1943

Dear Uncle Bill,

What a difficult year this must have been for you!

I understand you spent most of the year aboard the USS Patterson. Always you were in the thick of the fighting in the Pacific, back and forth between Australia and the Sea of Solomon. Your ship's job was to destroy Japanese airplanes as well as to rescue sailors from damaged vessels. There was scarcely a calm day without one or two battles.

It seems your days of fighting ended, however, when your ship had two problems in one day. First, Kamikazes — Japanese fighters who would do something brave even though it meant death — drove their airplane straight into your ship. It seems they always dive for the boiler room, which is again where you were — and you were this time seriously injured with shrapnel, flying bits of metal from the impact when the plane hit. You were badly injured . . . but your life was spared.

As I write this Christmas letter, you are in a hospital in Australia but it sounds like you'll be arriving back in America soon. There is a navy hospital in Virginia that will be taking care of you during recovery. Wish we could go see you there! I know Maxine, your girlfriend, is ready to leave to be with you.

Mama says we should share news from at home with you. Marvin is now 1½ years old and John is almost 3. Dorothy helps Mama with them more than I do since I have to help more with outside chores. I graduated from eighth grade and now stay home full time.

How war changes things!
Katherine Kroontje

"A (sister) is made for the day of adversity."

Chapter 12. Spring Vacation, 1944

Dorothy's Worst Memory *)

"Katherine, will you comb Dorothy's hair?" Mama called.

"Soon as I wash my hands," Katherine responded. "I just finished milking and they're smelly."

It was Thursday morning, the week of spring vacation. There was no school from Thursday through Monday, for five whole days.

"I don't need Katherine to comb my hair!" Dorothy raised her eyebrows defiantly. "Do you think I'm a baby? I'm almost ten years old, thank you!" Grabbing the comb, she began to yank through her shoulder length hair.

Mama and Katherine both laughed.

"All right then," Mama chuckled, "but you won't be able to have your hair braided or anything. It'll just have to be combed straight today."

"It's too short to stay in a braid, anyway!" Dorothy's lips set in a determined pout. "I like my hair straight like the other girls. So there!"

It was the last time anyone tried to comb Dorothy's hair. From then on, she fixed her own hair the way she wanted it fixed — straight to her shoulders.

*   *   *

---

* See Postlude for Historical Accuracy

Gerrit and Dorothy were the only Kroontjes in school in 1944. Willie and Katherine stayed home to help after they graduated from eighth grade at age 12. John was only three and Marvin only two years old, both too young for school.

Although Dorothy was the younger of the two school-aged children, she was always determined. She studied hard and did well in her classes. Katherine never opposed Papa when he said she must quit school after eighth grade. Papa said quit, so she quit. Had she continued school, Papa would have had to drive her to school and pick her up from school in Rock Rapids, eight miles away. But she often whispered to Dorothy that she *wished* she could go on and become a teacher.

*   *   *

It was 2:30 Thursday afternoon. Morning chores were long finished. Afternoon chores would be in two hours. The children had an hour to themselves.

Without waiting a second — lest Mama think up another chore — Katherine grabbed Dorothy's hand and they began to run towards the back pasture. Willie was helping Papa with farm chores but Gerrit joined the girls.

The back pasture was often a meeting place for neighborhood children with time to play.

"I hope those meanie boys don't join us today," commented Dorothy.

"They love to tease, don't they?" Gerrit agreed.

Katherine chuckled. "Remember the time they rode our bikes into the vegetable garden?"

"I definitely do!" replied Dorothy. "They borrowed our bikes and rode them down the hill over there. They didn't realize the bikes had no brakes."

Gerrit continued. "They rode down the hill as fast as they could. When they got near the garden, they couldn't stop because the brakes didn't work!"

Dorothy finished. "And so they rode through the fence. Right through it! They wrecked the fence and a whole patch of Mama's vegetable garden."

Katherine remembered. "I couldn't believe how calm Mama was about it. She had worked hard on those tomatoes and didn't like seeing them wrecked. But she was relieved that the boys didn't get hurt."

Gerrit added, "Papa was more upset. He had to fix the fence."

Dorothy sighed as she said, "I just hope the boys are fun today."

"Yeah," agreed Gerrit. "That's why we're here. For *fun!*"

*   *   *

Approaching the back fence, they saw that "those boys" were indeed there today. So were several other neighborhood children. It might be an enjoyable hour . . . if those neighbor boys didn't spoil things.

"Let's play by the bridge, okay?" Gerrit suggested. "Let's catch crayfish!"

"I'd rather wade," Katherine said. Dorothy agreed, since wading would cool her off. It was a warm day. Everyone agreed and headed for the bridge.

"Think you own the bridge?" teased one of "those boys."

"Why would I think that?" Gerrit answered quietly. "The bridge belongs to the government; anyone can play there."

Katherine could sense trouble brewing.

"Gerrit and Dorothy, let's go home right now," she whispered.

The whisper was too loud. The boys heard her.

"Go home?" the first boy taunted. "You're a sissy? Can't stand it when someone tells you the truth?"

"The truth?" Gerrit responded hotly. "You want the truth? The truth is that you boys are making trouble! We come here for a peaceful hour of play and you wreck it!"

"Let's just go," Katherine said again. "Ignore these trouble makers."

"Yah, yah," the first boy jeered at her. "Run home to Mama."

That was it. Katherine knew it. But she was too late to stop Dorothy.

Dorothy picked up a rock from under the bridge. Not a pebble, but a good-sized stone. With all her might, she flung the rock right at the boy speaking. No one was going to jeer at her sister!

The boy saw it coming. He ducked.

But his little brother hadn't been expecting it, so he got hit instead.

It hit him hard. Blood began spurting instantly from a wound in his forehead. He began screaming while he tried to stop the blood.

"Dorothy!" Katherine exclaimed, frightened. "What have you done? You go on home, *now! Now!*"

Dorothy didn't need a second warning. She ran.

"I'll be right back," Katherine told the boys. She followed Dorothy.

*   *   *

Dorothy's face was flushed as they approached the house.

"I didn't mean to hurt him!" she sputtered. "And it hit the wrong boy!"

"I'm sorry, Dorothy," Katherine panted as she continued running. "I'll get rags to stop the bleeding."

"I hope they don't tease you like that again," Dorothy responded, still upset. "I didn't want to hurt them but I do *not* like their teasing!"

"Mama says always turn the other cheek, you know," Katherine said. " 'We shouldn't make trouble,' she always tells us."

"I'm *not* making the trouble," Dorothy retorted. "*They* are. If we stand up to them once, maybe they'll quit making trouble, right? Yes, right!"

*   *   *

Fortunately, Mama was in the bedroom with the baby and didn't see them run into the kitchen.

"Quick!" Katherine whispered, "We need rag strips!"

Katherine grabbed the scissors while Dorothy found old rags and held them taut. Katherine cut them into strips.

Mama never heard them at all.

*   *   *

The boys were still at the bridge when Katherine returned. The wound was bad, blood still spurting. The boy was sobbing.

"Hold still," Katherine demanded, "and I'll stop that bleeding."

Surprisingly, the boy didn't say anything.

Katherine took the rag strips and wrapped them securely around the boy's head. It looked like a war wound, strips around and around the head. Finally the bleeding quit. Katherine tied the ends of the bandages securely together.

"There!" Katherine said. "Now go home and see if you can watch your tongue next time, okay? We want to play peacefully, right?"

The boys said nothing. Nothing at all.

*   *   *

"Hootah!" Katherine whistled to Gerrit as they walked back home. "Will Dorothy be in trouble now! Think the boys will tell Papa and Mama?"

"If they do, they'll be in trouble, too, don't you think?" answered Gerrit. "They've been pestering the life out of us. I've told them a bunch of times to quit.

"But she didn't really react until they attacked *you*, Katherine. She kind of idolizes her big sister, you know.

"I sort of think Dorothy is justified. Something had to be done!"

*   *   *

All Thursday evening, the children worried. Nothing happened.

All Friday, they worried. Nothing happened.

On Good Friday they hardly dared go to church. But the boys didn't go to their church so they weren't there to tattle.

By Monday, the last holiday, everyone figured it was over.

Dorothy was unusually subdued, however. She felt awful about hurting the smaller child. And Katherine knew she still worried. She knew only too well what would happen if anyone told Papa and Mama. They never allowed fighting.

Katherine figured since Monday was the last day of spring vacation, it was time for a special game to help Dorothy relax.

*   *   *

For some time, Katherine had been planning a surprise. This was the day for it — a surprise to help Dorothy forget her worry.

A few months earlier, Mama had bought the girls cut-out paper dolls. Anything store-bought was special, so they loved those paper dolls. They had made several sets of cut-out clothes for the dolls. They had drawn, colored, and cut out jumpers and blouses, socks and shoes, fancy hats, long party dresses, and coats . . . even jeans and boots so they could pretend the dolls had to do chores.

The dolls did everything the Kroontjes did in real life as well as everything they wished they could do.

It was fun to pretend — like living in a world of magic.

Katherine's "surprise" was to make the dolls come to life by adding pretty hair. She had asked Mama for strips of yellow wallpaper from wallpapering. Mama didn't think she'd need them again so agreed to let Katherine have them.

Now, on Monday afternoon with chores caught up, they had a few hours of free time. So Katherine called Dorothy upstairs for her surprise.

Taking out the paper dolls, Dorothy was already excited. She loved playing make-believe with those dolls. What they couldn't dream up!

Katherine shared her new idea.

Using Mama's scissors, they carefully cut the wallpaper into narrow strips of paper. They wrapped the strips around a pencil. Next they got the paper a little bit wet so it would stick to the pencil and pretty soon the wallpaper became long golden curls. Carefully removing the curls from the pencils, they used flour and water to make glue to attach the golden curls to the paper dolls.

It took a few tries to get it right — but then, what pretty dolls they had!

"Oh, Katherine, the curls on your doll are so pretty!" exclaimed Dorothy.

"I think your curls look the best," Katherine complimented her back.

"I wonder how the dolls would look with straight hair," Dorothy said, her eyes slanted upwards in contemplation.

Remembering that Dorothy wanted her hair straight, Katherine laughed.

"I don't think straight hair would work on the dolls," she replied merrily. "It would just look like yellow wallpaper then, don't you think?"

Secretly, what pleased Katherine most was that Dorothy relaxed and lost her look of fear. The distraction had worked.

*   *   *

To the relief of all the children, Papa and Mama never did learn about the stone throwing. At least, the children never heard about it.

"What do you think, Gerrit?" asked Katherine one day.

"I think those boys didn't dare tell what happened," Gerrit replied.

"What do you think they told their parents?" asked Katherine.

"Well," Gerrit improvised, "maybe the boys said they were running, slipped, and fell, right? That could explain it. And no one is in trouble!"

Whatever happened, for Dorothy it all turned out okay. Except that she always felt bad that it happened and that she hurt the younger boy.

From then on, the boys were fun to play with.

Papa and Mama never knew what happened.

"Behold, how great a matter a little fire kindleth!"

Chapter 13. May, 1944

Gerrit's Worst Memory

It was the day Gerrit played a childish prank.
It was the day Gerrit showed adult courage.

It is a day of which Gerrit is still embarrassed.
It is too honorable a memory to be forgotten . . .

*   *   *

In a day when there weren't many toys, each toy was a treasure.

Katherine's favorite toy was a doll, given to her at Christmas by Grandma Tilstra. The doll had a beautiful, painted-on face, shiny like porcelain, with painted-on hair. It was made . . . well, not of straw, but of stuffed material. To a girl who had never before owned a store-bought doll, it was a treasure.

The doll reminded Katherine of "Jeannie with the light brown hair" in the song so popular on the radio right then . . . so Katherine named her Jeannie. Jeannie had light brown hair, bright blue eyes, and a scarlet, rosebud mouth.

Often when Katherine had a bit of spare time, she would head for her bedroom and sit awhile with Jeannie. She would sit in the white-painted bay window. With Mama's gauzy, organza curtains and lace edging, the window was her favorite spot. There was enough room in the double bay window to squeeze in with the doll on her lap.

Katherine would sing little ditties to the doll, pretending Jeannie could sing along. Other times, she would read to her. If it was bedtime, she would cover Jeannie with a blanket and leave her, asleep, in her spot in the bay window.

Having Jeannie was like having her own pretend baby.

*   *   *

School assignments often involved research. One of eleven-year-old Gerrit's assignments was to write up the history of matchbooks. He was to read it for the final program of the school year.

Gerrit let Katherine read his finished assignment. This is what he wrote:

> *I have collected many matchbooks. To understand them, you must know how matches were invented.*
>
> *A match needs a chemical that can go on fire when rubbed.*
>
> *The first such chemical was <u>phosphorus</u>, discovered in 1669.*
>
> *In 1827, John Walker figured out that you could coat wood with <u>sulfur</u>, then start a fire by rubbing the stick. But his match smelled bad.*
>
> *In 1830, a Frenchman made a match with <u>white phosphorus</u>. But white phosphorus is poisonous and made people sick.*
>
> *In 1855, a man in Sweden made a match with <u>red phosphorus</u>. It was safe at last, but hard to make and expensive.*
>
> *In 1889, an American named Joshua Pusey invented the <u>matchbook</u>. About the same time, the Diamond Match Company also invented a matchbook. They bought Pusey's patent for $4,000 and then gave him a job.*
>
> *Matchbooks used cheap materials and were safe. They could be sold for pennies, so anyone could buy them.*
>
> *From 1935 to 1937, companies used matchbooks to advertise. They put neat things on them, like pictures of*

baseball players, and gave them away. It became cool to collect matchbooks.

Most matchbooks advertise the company that makes them. Some of mine advertise Diamond Match Company or Swedish Match Company.

But you have to <u>be</u> <u>careful</u> with matchbooks. They contain real matches and matches start real fires.

Katherine thought this was a perfect assignment for Gerrit. He was always watching for door to door salesmen who gave away matchbooks. When Papa took him to town, he was always watching, too. He had quite a collection!

*   *   *

Bedrooms were private spots. Girls never went into a boy's room. Boys never went into a girl's room. Gerrit — usually — stayed out of the girls' room.

But Gerrit was a normal boy. He loved to tease his sisters.

Today he felt like pulling a prank.

Knowing the girls were both busy downstairs, Gerrit went into the girls' bedroom. He looked around, curious to see what he might see.

On Katherine's dresser, near the window, he saw a box of matches.

Gerrit knew why the matches were there. They were used to light the kerosene lamps. The lamps were left on the dressers or else on the window ledges during the day. When it was time for bed, the girls would strike a match, light the kerosene lamps, and have light to get ready for bed.

Sometimes, they might read a while before going to sleep. Before climbing into bed, they would blow out the lamps.

On the dresser was a little porcelain box in which burned out matches were placed. If smoke was still in the matches, it would soon die out.

Gerrit lit a match just for fun. When the fire almost hit his finger, he blew it out and dropped the burnt match into the porcelain box.

*   *   *

Suddenly, Gerrit had an idea. He could play a trick!

He pulled a used match out of the porcelain box. He assumed the match was totally burned out.

The window needed cleaning. It was covered with a dewy film from burning the kerosene lamp every night. The film was perfect for Gerrit's purpose.

On the window ledge were two items: Katherine's beloved doll, and an open suitcase of clothes belonging to Jennie Kracht, the hired lady.

Taking the match, Gerrit knelt between the doll and suitcase, and began to write on the filmy window. Pressing hard, he slowly wrote, "Katherine loves . . ."

That was as far as he got before he received a big shock. The match he had thought was burned out suddenly burst into life — into a quick, bright flame. Within seconds, the flimsy organza of the curtains caught on fire.

Gerrit turned as white as the painted bed frames.

WHAT HAD HE DONE? WHAT HAD HE DONE?

*   *   *

To his great credit, it never even occurred to Gerrit to run and hide. He knew that fire had to be put out immediately and he couldn't do it himself.

Frantic, he ran to the stairway and down, down the stairs.

"M-Mom! Mom! M-Mom!" he called. He had become a little boy again. He was scared out of his wits, so scared he was stuttering.

"M-Mom! F-Fire! Fire! F-Fire!"

Mama, working on making supper, heard his frantic voice and knew it was serious. Instantly, she dropped her work and flew up the stairs. Up — up — up . . .

Now that Mama was in action, Gerrit disappeared outside.

*   *   *

By the time Mama reached the girls' bedroom, the organza curtains were blazing. The open suitcase, full of Jennie Kracht's clothes, was smoldering.

Katherine had followed Mama up the stairs. Her hand went to her mouth as she saw poor little Jeannie lying on the window ledge in the midst of all the heat from the fire. Jeannie was not burning but melting from the heat.

Would the whole bedroom go up in flames?

*   *   *

Mama had no water so she grabbed the first thing she saw. She pulled a sheet off of Katherine's bed.

With the sheet, she attacked the fire. She hit . . . and hit . . . and hit . . . Katherine, watching from behind the bed, dared get no closer.

*   *   *

Mama was gasping by the time the last bit of fire was put out. She had put it out all by herself! Katherine thought her a real heroine.

But then, Mama sat down on the bed and covered her face. She was shaking. She needed a few minutes to quit gasping and gain control again.

Meanwhile, Katherine walked around Mama and peered at the window. Most of the paint on the bay window had buckled and peeled. Not much was left of the lacy curtains, only ashes which had fluttered down to the ledge. And half of Jennie Kracht's clothes were scorched. What a mess!

Katherine was most upset about Jeannie. Poor Jeannie! All her skin was blistered and scorched. She couldn't be fixed.

Ho! That Gerrit was so naughty!

Where was he, anyway?

*   *   *

Katherine never saw how Papa dealt with Gerrit. When he came in for supper, he was sobbing. While everyone else ate Mama's tasty supper, he choked on his food.

After supper Papa often chose supper devotions that fit something special which had happened. Tonight he opened his Bible to *James 3*. Looking at everyone around the table, Papa read slowly, *"In many things, we offend all."*

That didn't seem fair. Papa was looking at everyone else, as though they had done something wrong! He wasn't even looking at Gerrit.

Papa read about putting bits in horses' mouths so they would obey.

He read about huge ships being controlled in hurricanes with a tiny wheel.

And he read about a little fire bursting into a huge fire. "Yes!" Katherine thought. "That's what Gerrit did! With a little match, he made a huge fire . . ."

But Papa continuing reading . . . and now he wasn't talking about Gerrit.

"Even so the tongue is a little member . . .
"And the tongue is a fire, a world of iniquity . . . it is set on fire
of hell . . .
"The tongue can no man tame . . .
"Therewith bless we God . . . and therewith curse we men . . .
"Out of the same mouth proceedeth blessing and cursing!
"My brethren, these things ought not so to be!
"The wisdom that is from above is first pure, then peaceable,
gentle . . .
"Righteousness is sown in peace of them that make peace."

"Children," Papa said, before the prayer of thanksgiving, "Gerrit made a mistake today. He played a prank, wanting to tease you girls. That wasn't kind.

"Gerrit paid for his mistake. He didn't expect to have a fire; he certainly didn't try to start that! His mischief resulted in much more than he thought.

"But Gerrit is sorry for his mistake. Now it is our turn to do what is right.

"Are we going to let our words be words of cursing? Or of blessing? Can we forgive Gerrit for a mistake he didn't intend?

"Or will we have a worse fire in our family? A fire of words? Of anger?"

*   *   *

Lying in bed, Katherine found herself unable to sleep. The sulfur smell of fire was still strong in the air. And Papa's words at supper burned in her heart.

Why had Papa sounded like everybody else had more guilt than Gerrit? After all, Gerrit had started that fire! He was to blame!

*   *   *

Just then Katherine heard a sound on the other side of the wall. Listening closely, she realized that the sound was Gerrit. Gerrit wasn't sleeping, either. He was crying!

Gerrit's sobs were heart-wrenching. Katherine didn't want to hear them.

At first she tried to ignore the crying. But then she remembered Papa's devotions: *"The wisdom that is from above is . . . peaceable, gentle . . ."*

And Katherine knew what she had to do.

*   *   *

"Gerrit . . . Gerrit . . ."

Katherine's whisper from his bedside shocked Gerrit. Never before had Katherine entered his bedroom when he was in bed!

"Gerrit, may I say something?"

"Wh — what, Katherine?"

"Gerrit, I think it was real brave of you to 'fess up to what you did today."

Although Katherine couldn't see his face in the dark, she heard Gerrit's surprised intake of breath. He had thought everyone condemned him completely!

"I'm sorry, Katherine," he sobbed. "I'm real' sorry about your doll. I didn't mean to start a fire. It . . . it happened so fast!"

"I know, Gerrit. You didn't mean for it to happen," agreed Katherine. "And you were brave, too, Gerrit. Think what would have happened if you hadn't told Mama right away. The fire could have burned down the whole house!

"Mama was able to put out the fire . . . because you told her, right away.

"Thank you, Gerrit. Thank you for being brave enough to tell Mama!"

"But Katherine," Gerrit sobbed, "your pretty gift from Grandma is all ruined. Grandma will think me terribly naughty. I was only trying to tease!"

"I know, Gerrit. Promise me you won't tease me again about boys? If you won't tease me about boys, then I won't tease you about the fire. Deal?"

To Katherine's surprise, she suddenly found Gerrit hugging her.

"Thank you, Katherine. You're the best sister a boy could have!"

*   *   *

Back in bed again, Katherine still ached for her doll Jeannie. But she felt an even stronger emotion. She thought about it for a moment. There was only one word for this new emotion. It was *peace*.

Yes, *peace*. She felt peace with God and with Gerrit and with Papa. Because she had done the right thing. The thing God wanted.

And now she realized it was true: Gerrit had been brave. What if he had run away and denied that he started the fire? What then?

His bravery had saved the house! Gerrit, too, was a hero!

"He that loveth his brother abideth in the light . . ."

John Cecil by Little Yellow House, 1943

Chapter 14. July, 1944

Katherine's Worst Memory

"Willie! Katherine! Gerrit! Dorothy! Time for chores . . ."

Papa's voice, nasally in the morning, broke into Katherine's dreams. She had dreamed about the county fair to be held next week. In her dream, she worried about whether to enter blackberry or rhubarb jam. Now, rubbing her eyes, Katherine grinned. Why, she hadn't made either jam yet!

Streaming through the half-open bedroom door, early morning sunlight turned the wooden bedroom floor a golden haze. Squinting, Katherine watched the light play games with the bed quilt over her toes.

The sunlight hit Katherine's left hand on the edge of the bed. Spreading her fingers wide, she stared, fascinated, at veins forming on her hands. Obviously, her hands were not a city girl's milky white, smooth hands. They were hands of a farm girl, accustomed to work. Three raised veins proved that.

Katherine had seen Willie admire the veins in his hands because they made him feel like a man. But Katherine wished her hands were more like those in the *Ladies' Home Journal*. Those ladies had smooth, tapered hands. Katherine only had time to clip her nails once a week, never time to file them.

"Katherine!" Papa's voice was grouchy now. "Are you and Dorothy up?"

"Yes, Pa! I'll be down in two minutes . . ."

Prodding Dorothy awake, Katherine pulled on her faded gingham dress. She met Willie and Gerrit on the landing and the three of them trooped downstairs together. Dorothy, so quick in the daytime, was still "rubbing cobwebs from her eyes." She followed in a few minutes.

Grabbing milk pails off the porch, Katherine and Gerrit headed for the barn. Breakfast was at 7:30. Mama would scurry around the house, getting little ones dressed and breakfast on the table. Papa and Willie cared for the horses and prepared to go to the fields. Gerrit and she did the milking.

Dorothy, almost ten years old now, helped Mama in the house. She dressed three-year-old John and two-year-old Marvin. Since it was hot weather, the toddlers wore little shorts around the house. Dorothy must also have the beds made up and the upstairs neat before breakfast.

*   *   *

By now, Katherine could milk a cow as well as anyone. Seated on a stool in a stall on the right side of the barn, the rising sun providing shadowy light, milking was as natural as breathing.

Cats lined the stalls, waiting for their breakfast.

Squirt! Aha, her aim was accurate. Katherine aimed the milk almost without thought into a cat's open mouth. Not one drop was wasted.

Nor was one second wasted.

Squirt! Milk shot into a second cat's open mouth.

Squirt! Squirt! Into the milk pail.

Squirt! Into a third cat's mouth.

Squirt! Squirt! Squirt! Into the milk pail.

Katherine's hands kept up a steady rhythm. The milk pail rapidly filled up. She could milk cows almost as fast as Papa now. Maybe even faster. That's why Papa could be out with the horses, getting ready for fieldwork.

*   *   *

The final cow was milked. Gerrit would put the cows into the pasture, clean out gutters, and hand-crank a pail of corn for the pig trough.

Katherine's next chore was carrying the milk pails into the summer kitchen to separate the milk from the cream. This, too, had to be finished before breakfast at 7:30.

Anyone who could turn the crank could run the separator. Dorothy came running into the summer house as Katherine set down the last pail. "May I help?" she pleaded, her eyes eager. Dorothy didn't often help with separating.

"Are you finished helping Mama?" asked Katherine.

"Of course! John and Marvin are both in their high chairs, ready for breakfast. Mama told me to come help you."

With the two girls working together, the separating went faster. Katherine poured raw milk into the large shiny bowl at the top of the separator. Dorothy turned the crank, causing skimmed milk to spurt from one faucet into a pail and cream to squish through another faucet into another pail. Skimmed milk would be fed to the hogs . . . and also, once a week, Mama would make cheese from it.

As Katherine moved the full pail of skimmed milk to the side, replacing it with an empty pail before any milk splattered on the floor, she sighed with satisfaction. Just thinking of Mama's cheese made it worth the work of separating the milk. No one made better cheese than Mama. It was delicious!

*   *   *

Oatmeal. Eggs. Milk. Bacon. Bread. A typical breakfast. Tasty and nourishing. No one ever complained. They had already worked up an appetite and the food tasted wonderful.

Sometimes, in town at the grocery store, Katherine would page through city magazines and marvel at breakfasts in rich people's homes. They had all sorts of strange foods: orange juice, waffles, pancakes, hash browns, and white bread, among other things. Sometimes they even had steaks for breakfast! Katherine knew Mama would never have time to fix all that. Plus, where would they buy oranges for orange juice? No, they ate only what they could raise on the farm.

But their food was more than enough.

When Papa thanked God for supplying them with daily bread and much more, Katherine felt thankful.

*   *   *

Dishes were finished in record time. With hot, soapy water from dishes still in the large bowl, the girls' next job was to clean the cream separator parts.

Cleaning the separator was more work than breakfast dishes. All the discs from the separator had to be taken into the kitchen and put into hot soapy water. Milk doesn't come off easily so the discs had to be carefully scrubbed until clean, then rinsed. Water was always hot on the stove to be added to dish water as needed. Katherine washed the separator parts; Dorothy dried them.

"This takes so long!" complained Dorothy, her eyebrows lowered.

"Yes," agreed Katherine, "but think of Mama's cheese!"

"Yummy," agreed Dorothy. "I guess it's worth it, then."

"And Mama can sell the cream," added Katherine.

"Yep, then we might buy a new dress for Christmas." That thought made the work worthwhile. A pretty new dress would be a delight.

*   *   *

Dorothy's next job was to watch John and Marvin. She took them outside to play.

Katherine, meanwhile, had to feed the chickens. After bringing the clean separator discs into the summer kitchen, she headed for the granary.

"Dorothy!" Mama called from the house. "Can you come here? I need you to run to the cellar."

Since Mama was calling Dorothy, Katherine paid no attention. She continued walking to the granary. She didn't notice that, with Dorothy answering Mama's call, little John was now following her.

In the granary, Katherine scooped up a large shovelful of oats and corn mixed together. Her job was to toss the grain out the door, scattering it around so the chickens could scratch and peck it for their breakfast.

Concentrating on her job, Katherine did not notice John only a few feet behind her. She turned swiftly with the full scoop, swinging it backward and then forward to scatter grain around the yard.

"Ow-w-w!" came an anguished scream from behind her.

Katherine's eyes opened in horror. Was little John there? Oh my! She had hit him with that scoop! Blood was spurting all over.

"John!" screamed Katherine. "John, why were you out here?"

But this was no time to ask questions. Katherine grabbed John and ran as fast as she could to the house. Blood spurted from the gash in his forehead. Blood was getting all over both of them.

Katherine was terrified.

"Mama! Papa!" she screamed as loudly as she could. "Mama! Papa!"

For the moment, Katherine was no longer the capable, strong girl who could milk as well as Papa and clean a separator as well as Mama. She was a child needing her parents' help. She needed help for her little brother, whom she loved so dearly.

Dorothy came rushing back up from the cellar.

Mama came rushing from the kitchen.

Papa came running from the barn.

"Mama! Papa!" Katherine babbled, sobbing almost hysterically. "Take John to the doctor! He needs stitches!"

Papa grabbed a clean rag and wiped the blood running down John's face.

"Katherine, calm down," Papa said quietly. "Let's see how bad this is before we waste all morning going to the doctor."

John was also crying, but not as hard as Katherine.

"Pa, look at all that blood!" sobbed Katherine. "It's everywhere!"

Papa, still wiping away the blood, shook his head. "It isn't that serious, Katherine," he responded. He couldn't afford time to head to town unless it was absolutely necessary.

Mama meanwhile found iodine and bandages. She doused a cloth with iodine and held it to John's wound. Then he really howled! That made Katherine howl louder along with him. Her hands covered her eyes as she wept with and for little John.

Mama's hands continued to dab the iodine on John.

"Katherine, what happened?" Mama asked.

"I don't know," sobbed Katherine. "I had no idea he was out there behind me. I would never, never hurt him on purpose."

"I'm sure you wouldn't try to hurt him," Mama responded gently. "It was my fault for calling Dorothy into the house. I should have warned you."

At last the bleeding slowed down. Mama was able to cover it with salve and a tight bandage. The bandage covered John's whole forehead above his eye. It didn't make Katherine feel at all better.

"Now, John, you must lie down until this quits bleeding," Mama commanded. She carried him into the house and laid him on her own bed so he could be nearby where she could check on him occasionally.

"And you, Katherine," Mama added as she came back from her bedroom, "take off those bloody clothes and soak them in cold water. This afternoon you can wash out the blood. Put on a pair of Gerrit's overalls to finish chores."

Then Mama pulled Katherine into a warm hug.

"Get hold of yourself, Girl. These things happen. No one blames you!"

*   *   *

Katherine sobbed the entire time she finished feeding the hens. Although everyone felt sorry for little John, they felt almost as sorry for Katherine. She couldn't believe she had given her baby brother that wound.

John's forehead bled off and on all afternoon. Mama replaced bandages every time blood seeped out of them. John had to lie down all day.

By next morning, the bleeding had stopped. Within a week, the sore healed and the bandages came off. In a month, the sore became a scar.

Although the scar gradually lightened, it remained on John's forehead all his life. Still today, as we write this story, that scar remains over John's right eye.

John never held it against Katherine. He forgave her immediately.

But Katherine never forgot. It remained her worst memory from the little yellow house . . .

Because she really did love her little brother!

Christmas Letter 1944

Dear Uncle Bill,

In May, 1943, I graduated from eighth grade. I wrote that last year. I was twelve years old, almost thirteen. But I continue making the war scrapbook we began in school shortly after the Pearl Harbor attack.

We counted the countries involved in this war. Fifty countries! We studied maps, too. Continents: Europe, North Africa and Asia. Oceans: Atlantic, Pacific, Indian Oceans and the Mediterranean Sea. Wow!!

But for you, the war is over. At least your part in it is. You have spent the year being treated for your injuries at the navy hospital in Virginia. All that time, Maxine was out there encouraging you.

And just think, three days after Christmas you and Maxine will be married! We all really wish we could be there but it's impossible. With the war effort, we have to preserve everything, especially tires. But we'll be praying for you and Maxine and desire God's blessing on your marriage.

Even though your part in the war is over, you remain our hero, Uncle Bill. You served God and our country faithfully while in the war and helped save many lives, including the lives of your own friends.

We are praying that God will help you overcome the shell shock which you still suffer. I can well imagine the awful memories.

Remembering you all the time, and thankful that God spared your life,

Your niece,
Katherine Kroontje

"Faithful are the wounds of a friend . . ."

_____

_____

_____

_____

_____

"Papa! Stop it! You are killing me!"

Chapter 15. April, 1945

Papa Cuts Out a Sliver

For April, which can be cold and blustery, it was a gorgeous day. The sun high in the sky produced record temperatures in the seventies. What could go wrong on such a beautiful April day?

Katherine whistled during her milking. She sang as she separated the cream. She was cheerful as she helped Dorothy and Gerrit off to school. They had only a month left at school before summer vacation. Then four children would be at home to help Papa and Mama.

It was amazing how much cheer a little sun could bring.

With the children gone to school, breakfast dishes finished, and the cream separator cleaned, Katherine's next job was the chickens. She had to feed the hens, as always. After that, clean out hen house nests. This job was done once a month or so, whenever the straw seemed too dirty for the chickens.

*   *   *

The hen house on this second farm was a nice building. It was roughly 12 feet by 15 feet in size. It was sort of like two rectangles, half of it 12' x 7½' and the other half another 12' x 7½'.

The one end had little sticks sticking straight out from the wall, with chicken wire laid over the sticks. This was a place where hens could "roost" when they weren't in their nests.

The other end had little cubicles on the wall, like a huge bookcase with many divisions on each shelf. Each cubicle was a square, one foot by one foot. Straw was put into each cubicle to make a nest in which a hen could lay eggs.

Altogether there were around one hundred hens. That is a lot of hens! Not all of them laid eggs at the same time, but still, there were a lot of nests to go through when looking for eggs.

And now, today, all those nests had to be cleaned out.

Katherine usually didn't mind the job. It would take the rest of the morning, and a noon meal would be waiting when she finished. It was a job she could do alone and one she knew well. After all, she did it every month.

*   *   *

The first part of the job was to bring fresh straw into the building.

That meant going to the large pile of straw in the yard. Using a pitchfork, Katherine scooped up as large a heap of straw as she could handle. She carried this scoop to the chicken house and dropped it just outside the door.

Katherine cleaned the empty cubicles first, because they were easy to clean with no hens sitting in them. It didn't take long at all to reach into each nest and swipe out the dirty straw onto the floor. Later, Papa would use the pitchfork to scoop up this dirty straw, carry it to the doorway, and make a pile a few feet from the chicken house. Papa did it because dirty straw was heavy.

Next, Katherine carried in the pile of clean straw, again using the pitchfork. This was normally about the right amount of straw for the empty nesting cubicles. For each nest, she grabbed a generous amount of straw for a fluffy nest to please the mother hen, then spread it roughly but evenly in the cubicle. Now hens could come when they wanted and lay eggs in clean nests.

*   *   *

No, cleaning out the *empty* cubicles was no problem.

The tricky part was cleaning out the nests of the hens sitting on their eggs.

Hens on eggs didn't like to be disturbed. They were called *"broetse kippen"* ("broody hens") because they were "brooding" — keeping eggs warm so chicks could hatch. They didn't like it when someone took their eggs in the morning. They also didn't like it when Katherine tried to clean out their nests.

Whistling while she worked, Katherine nonetheless kept a close eye on the broody hens. She already had scars from those hens! She didn't need more.

Using a stick, Katherine prodded a hen from her nest.

"Out, Mama!" she said cheerfully. "Just a minute or two, okay? You want a nice clean nest, don't you?"

The hen squawked but flapped down anyway. She didn't like that stick.

Quickly Katherine swept out the dirty straw and replaced it with clean.

"Okay, Mama, you can go back in now," she grinned as she moved to the next nest and repeated the process.

Sometimes a hen went right back in as soon as Katherine moved on. Other times, a hen flew in a huff to the other end of the coop and sat on the roost. When Katherine was far away from her nest, she would return.

Some hens didn't return until she had the entire job finished.

And that was fine with her! She wished they'd all stay on the roost!

*   *   *

The sun was nearly overhead now; it was dinnertime. The timing was perfect, because Katherine was nearly finished with the chicken coop.

Katherine reached into the last nest. With a firm and practiced swipe, she pulled out all the straw in one swipe and threw it onto the floor. Papa would add it to the large, dirty pile in the yard.

There! Add a handful of clean straw, and the job was finished.

Elated, Katherine latched the chicken coop shut. Slipping the latch into place, she didn't notice a jagged sliver of wood sticking out of the wood near the latch. Until . . .

"OU-OU-OU-CH!"

All the joy of the finished job flew out of Katherine's mind as horrid pain stabbed her hand. The pain was as unbearable as it was unexpected. A long, sharp splinter of wood from the door had pierced under her third fingernail.

Katherine forgot all about the dinner waiting in the house.

"Papa! Papa! I need help!" Katherine screamed, flying out of the chicken yard, holding her throbbing finger to try to dull the pain.

She was too big to cry anymore — after all, she was now fourteen years old! But tears came anyway. It really, really hurt. Anyone would cry.

Fortunately, Papa was heading home from the fields for dinner. Hearing Katherine's screams, he came running. Had the sliver been a small one, he would have scolded her for screaming. But when he saw the thick size of the sliver, he was shocked himself.

"This must come out!" he exclaimed.

That made Katherine feel good. At least Papa was concerned.

"Sit right here," he commanded, pointing to the cellar doorway near the house. "I'll take care of that old sliver."

And, reaching into his back pocket, he pulled out something he always carried with him, his huge — gigantic, Katherine thought — pocketknife.

*   *   *

"Papa! Papa! Stop it! You are killing me!"

"Hush, Katherine, don't be a baby," Papa commanded as he concentrated on the sliver. His knife cut and cut, right under the fingernail, as he tried to get in far enough to pull out the sliver.

Katherine tried to pull her hand away but Papa kept a firm hold with his left hand while he worked with his right hand.

"Hold still!"

"It h-hurts, Papa!" Katherine sobbed.

"I'm almost finished now. It's coming . . ." Papa said as he finally got the sliver to pull out.

"Don't move yet, Katherine," he said. "There may be dirt or leftover wood in there; you could get an infection. We must clean it."

Moving quickly into the house while Katherine sobbed on the flat cellar door, he returned in just a minute with Mama's big bottle of iodine.

"No, Papa, not iodine!" Katherine pleaded. It had been used on cuts before and she knew how it hurt. This was long before pharmaceutical companies produced "No sting, No Stain, Bactine," or, later yet, Hydrogen Peroxide.

"Yes, Katherine, the iodine!" Papa responded firmly.

Papa didn't do things halfway. Just as he did on an animal wound, he poured the iodine. A good, liberal pour to make sure no infection remained. He ignored Katherine's howls just as he would ignore a pig's squeals.

It hurt something awful. At eighty years of age, Katherine still recalled how awful that hurt. It may have been necessary, but Papa was no gentle doctor, that was for sure.

*   *   *

The April sun was still shining.

But the rest of the day, for Katherine, was one blur of pain.

She could hardly do *any* work. The jobs Mama found to keep her busy were easy but still difficult to do.

She also had to fight tears the whole time.

Finally Mama told her to take a nap. Trying not to cry since Mama was being kind, Katherine climbed the stairs and crawled under the quilt. The finger throbbed so badly that it took her an hour to fall asleep, but then exhaustion took over and she slept all afternoon.

Gradually, the finger improved. But it took a l-o-n-g time!

Katherine never forgot the day when Papa played doctor.

But she also never held it against him because she understood. Had he not removed that sliver, she could have gotten a bad infection and *actually* died.

Papa's pain was given in love.

"Faithful are the wounds of a friend . . ."

"There is nothing better for a man . . .
than that he should . . . enjoy good in his labor."

Chapter 16. October, 1945

Runaway Horses

"One hundred!" Katherine shouted.

"One hundred ten!" Willie shouted back.

"All right, you two, just work," Papa grunted.

It was the last week in October. The weather was cold but no snow had yet fallen. The job of the week was picking ears of field corn.

Willie and Katherine shared a wagon. Their job was to pick ears of corn off stalks, husk them, and throw them into the wagon. The wagon had a "bang board" on one side, a board which prevented ears from flying over the wagon and landing on the ground. A bang board saved a lot of time because they didn't have to be careful how they threw ears. They could toss an ear into the wagon; it would hit the bang board and fall into the wagon. Neat!

But after awhile, even the fun part of hitting the bang board dulled. Then Willie and Katherine made the job more fun by competing. It was fun to see who could pick and husk faster. Plus, the work seemed to get done faster.

Papa had a wagon all by himself. He was more experienced at picking, so he could pick almost as fast alone as the two of them picked together.

Since their counting bothered Papa, Willie and Katherine counted silently while he was in the field. When he pulled a load to the yard, they would count aloud again . . . until he was back in the field.

*   *   *

Katherine was now fifteen years old. She could do most field jobs just as well as any man. Picking corn was a familiar job, done every harvest season.

This wasn't sweet corn for people to eat. This was field corn for the animals. It had to get really dry before it was picked so it wouldn't spoil over the winter. While sweet corn was usually picked in August or September, field corn wasn't picked until late October or even November, depending how long it took to dry.

Really, although they called it "picking corn," they were doing two jobs at once. They were picking the corn and husking it at the same time. They would leave the husks in the field so they wouldn't have to make a mess in the yard.

Farmers always figured out ways to make work go easier and faster. For field corn husking, Papa had figured out a way to speed up the job. Each of them wore a special leather glove on his hand. Attached to the leather was a hook. The hook made stripping the husks off the corn go fast.

When Katherine helped Mama strip sweet corn, she would try to strip one ear every minute. That was about as fast as she could go getting off every single hair. But with field corn, they never worried about hairs because hairs didn't bother animals.

Not worrying about hairs when they stripped husks off field corn, it went much faster. She never had a clock to time herself but Katherine figured she could go about three times as fast. Maybe even four times as fast. Three to four ears per minute.

Competing against Willie was the way to make it fun . . . and faster.

*   *   *

Papa wasn't stripping husks close to Willie and Katherine but had his wagon up ahead. He could only hear them count when they shouted.

Attached to each wagon were two horses. Frank and Prince were attached to Papa's wagon. Molly and Topsy were attached to Willie and Katherine's wagon. The horses were usually mild mannered. They chomped on corn husks as they moved along, placidly chewing and spitting out whatever they didn't like. Corn husks were good fodder for them — a mix of fiber and corn, good for their stomachs.

While Papa picked corn, the reins for the horses were lying on the ground. Since the horses were calm, there was no need to tie them to a post. They waited patiently until Papa wanted them to move forward. To move them forward, Papa picked up the reins off the ground and gave a gentle tug, letting them know they had to move. Since the horses did this job every year, they knew what to expect and moved forward a few feet until Papa called out, "Whoa now!"

When either wagon was full, Papa took a break from picking corn and drove the wagon to the yard. He came back with an empty wagon. Often the two wagons were full at almost the same time, so he would pull one load, then the other, and then again begin picking corn.

Papa was a really fast corn picker!

Together, Willie and Katherine were faster — but not by much.

*   *   *

It was nearly mid-afternoon. Although the temperature was brisk, Katherine was sweating from the hard work. Willie had tied a bandana around his head to keep sweat out of his eyes.

"You still counting, Katherine?" Willie taunted her. "How many ears do you figure you've stripped so far today?"

"At least as many as you," she joked back. "How many have you stripped, Will?"

Willie chuckled.

"Well, I kind of quit counting a few hours ago, when Pa didn't like it," he responded. "But I've been doing some math. If I strip four ears a minute, that's 240 ears an hour. We've been at this around seven hours now, so I guess 240 times seven is nearly 1700 ears, eh? Think you've done 1700 ears yet?"

Katherine smirked, "Only 1700?? My, you're slow! I've done at least 2000!"

Will hooted in response. "Okay then, let's actually count while Pa brings in his next load, huh? We'll see who's faster, Smarty Pants!"

*   *   *

A mile over, a farmer was driving with his wagon full of corn. He had new, high-strung horses. The horses weren't used to the job of pulling wagons all day and didn't like the monotony of the job.

Suddenly, one of those horses reared and let out a high-pitched scream. That upset his partner, who also reared and let out a shrill neigh. The cold, clear air made the shrill neighs travel easily across the mile section.

Willie and Katherine, intent on their corn picking, scarcely noticed the sound. Papa heard, however, and stopped to listen. He knew one important thing: spooked horses spook other horses.

Immediately, Papa saw that Molly and Topsy, the two horses now on his wagon, were upset by the shrill neighing of the neighboring horses. Quickly, he jumped onto the wagon seat to calm the horses. But it was too late. The horses were already responding to the shrill neighing by neighing themselves. And then they began to run. There was no stopping them. They were far too excited.

The path that Molly and Topsy ran was the alleyway along the edge of the field. This was the path to and from the pastures which the cows usually walked. The spooked horses ran toward the yard, pulling the wagon, Papa on the seat, yelling to try to stop them. It would have been hilarious if it hadn't been so dangerous.

Willie and Katherine, watching what was happening, began to yell, too.

"Papa! Jump off! Jump off!" yelled Katherine. She was frightened.

Willie was yelling the same thing except using his abbreviation for Papa. "Pa! Pa! Jump off! Jump off!" he yelled.

The danger was obvious. The spooked horses could easily tip the wagon. If so, Papa could be injured or killed.

Seeing that he couldn't control the frightened animals, Papa finally did jump off. Although he stumbled and nearly fell, he landed safely in the cornfield. Katherine raced over to make sure he was okay.

Papa stood for a few seconds, shaking his head.

"Can't figure out how easily a horse can get spooked," he muttered. "Just when you think an animal is as dependable as an animal can be, it spooks.

"Well, guess we'd better head for the yard to calm them down."

*   *   *

The terrified horses raced to the yard, past the windmill. There, the wagon tipped, forcing them to stop. Corn spilled all over the yard. The horses tangled up in the harnesses.

What a mess!

When Katherine had run to help Papa, Willie had driven the second team of horses over to pick up Papa and Katherine, then drove them all to the yard.

Tying Frank and Prince to a post, Willie joined Papa in helping Molly and Topsy. They were now lying on the ground, all tangled up, unable to move. Their sides were heaving from the fright they had given themselves.

As Willie and Papa untangled the horses from the harnesses, Katherine heaved the strewn corn back into the wagon.

Papa knew it was useless to do anymore work today with those horses. Once spooked, horses need hours to calm down. So after the horses were untangled, Willie and he led them into the barn and began evening chores. The horses were rubbed down and taken care of so they wouldn't become sick.

Katherine finished picking up the corn mess and then she, too, followed them into the barn. Corn picking for that day was ended.

*   *   *

At suppertime, Papa remarked to Mama, "I'm surprised, Susie, that you never came outside to see what was happening."

To everyone's amazement, Mama responded, "What are you talking about, Wilbur? What happened?"

And while Mama heard the story and became upset, everyone else quit being upset and began to laugh . . . because Mama had heard nothing of the runaway horses!

Christmas Letter 1945

Dear Uncle Bill and Aunt Maxine,

The war is over! In Europe and in the Far East!

War with Germany ended in May. Church bells rang! It was announced in school! We went to Rock Rapids for a town parade and celebration.

Although we were thrilled about Europe, war with Japan continued. Month after month we heard about victories — but it took five more months to win.

In August, those awful atomic bombs dropped on Japan. Was that really necessary? Maybe, because in September the Japanese part of the war ended. Now it is over.

Meanwhile, last December 28, 1944, three days after Christmas, you two married each other — out there in Virginia, by the naval hospital. You still had to be in and out for treatment so you couldn't come out here for the wedding.

And this year, you moved to Minneapolis. Your address says Girard, Minneapolis, Hennepin, Minnesota. I'm not sure what the Hennepin means. Is it Hennepin County?

Will we see you at the Tilstra Reunion on Memorial Day?

Thankful the war is now over,
Katherine Kroontje

PART III: 1946 – 1948

Last Years in the Little Yellow House

. . .

and

. . .

The War is Over!

John and Marvin by Mama's Peonies in 1946

"The LORD gave . . . The LORD (taketh) . . .
Blessed be the name of the LORD."

Katherine in 1948

Chapter 17. July 14, 1946

Substitute Daughter

"Here comes Mrs. Latis!" Dorothy whispered to Katherine.

Church service had just ended on Sunday morning. Katherine was heading to visit with other girls outside the church. It looked like she might not make it there.

"Katherine!" Mrs. Latis' high-pitched, nervous voice was all sugar and honey. "Can I talk with you a minute, Dear?"

Inwardly, Katherine quaked. She might never get away from this lady.

Outwardly, she remained kind and composed. It was a duty to show courtesy. And the lady meant well. She just had pain she could never forget.

*   *   *

Every time Katherine saw Mrs. Latis, the horrible memory resurfaced.

The tragedy had occurred when Katherine was only a tike, four years old. She was still living in the Little White House, near Rock Rapids, two miles south of where she now lived.

Mr. and Mrs. Latis were neighbors living a half mile north and a half mile west. They had two sons, one a teenager and one ten years old. And they had one daughter, a cute and very curious little girl, the same age as Katherine.

The girl was adorable. She had bouncy brown hair, sometimes teased into curls. Since Katherine's thick hair was usually short and neat, she was fascinated by this girl's pretty, flouncy hair.

She was a girl who never sat still. If Katherine's family happened to sit behind the Latis family, she would see the little girl fidgeting most of the sermon. When the service was over, she would wriggle between people in the aisles and head for the grocery store owner who always had a piece of candy for little kids. She loved the lemon drops he carried in his pockets.

Katherine was the same age. She loved the little girl. But she never dared to ask for candy. She would stand shyly at a distance and merely hope he might notice her. He usually did . . . and she had her lemon drop, too.

*   *   *

The Tragedy occurred when the Latis' girl was four years old.

One of the older brothers was an inquisitive boy. He loved to tinker around with automobiles. But he wasn't allowed yet to do much with them.

It was a spring afternoon in 1934. Mrs. Latis was in the house preparing supper. Mr. Latis was in the field. He would soon be home to do evening chores with his two sons.

A year before, the Latis' parents had purchased a new car. They parked their older car, an off brand, in the orchard. They thought sometime they'd get rid of that car, maybe get a few dollars at a junk dealer. When winter snow covered the car, they forgot about it.

Forgetting was a fatal mistake.

The Latis' boy had not forgotten. And today was exactly the sort of day when an old car sitting in the orchard looked inviting.

First the boy climbed onto the seat of the car and pretended to be driving it. No harm there, right?

Then he decided to check whether the car still had any gasoline in it. He reached into his pocket and saw that among his other treasures he had matches. Only two of them, but two should be enough.

He would find out if there was any gasoline in that car's tank.

*   *   *

The ten-year-old boy slid to the ground and walked around the car to the gasoline tank. The tank's cap twisted hard because it was getting rusty but he managed to get it off. He sniffed. The smell wasn't strong but he did think there was a smell of gasoline.

Slowly he pulled one match from his pocket. Did he dare . . . ?

The temptation was too great. Yes, he dared! He had to know!

Raising his shoe, he struck the match and held it over the opening . . .

*　　*　　*

The ten-year-old hadn't noticed his four-year-old sister approaching. She was often his shadow during the day. She certainly found him more interesting than the adults.

Seeing her brother by the old car, the girl ran for all she was worth. Naturally inquisitive, she wanted to see what he was doing. Her eyes shone as she raced across the orchard. Once she stumbled on an apple tree root but she quickly recovered her balance and raced on.

The girl approached the car just as her brother struck the match. Without hesitation, she leaned over to watch. She guessed what he was doing and she, too, wanted to know if there was any gasoline in there.

How quickly it happened!

Both of them were unprepared for the horrific explosion. It wasn't just a small "Poof" — it was a gigantic explosion. No name does it justice.

The boy jumped quickly away. Even so, he received bad burns from the explosion on his hands, arms, and face.

But when he turned back to help his little sister, he was too late. The explosion had literally engulfed her. She was on fire all over and was killed within seconds.

It was a nightmare from which the boy never fully recovered.

*　　*　　*

Neighbors had been wonderful to the family. Mama had gone there every day for a week, bringing food and comfort. Neighbors from miles away drove there to help the distressed family. It was all anyone talked about.

Every time Mama went there, she took Katherine along. Katherine was too small to understand what had really happened. She heard adults talking and knew the pretty little girl had been killed by fire. It wasn't until she was older that the horror really sank in.

But one thing she knew. Every time Mama and she went over there, the girl's mama would be crying . . . *until she saw Katherine*. Then her eyes would light up. She would hold out her arms and say, "Oh, child! Come! Come!" And Katherine, being a toddler and responding to the warmth of an adult, would allow the lady to hug her. Usually the lady managed to find a cookie or a piece of candy and give it to her.

No one really saw anything strange when the lady asked Mama if Katherine could come over now and then to visit. Mama understood that she had lost her only daughter and that Katherine was the same age. *In the lady's mind, Katherine became her daughter's substitute.* Every time she saw Katherine, it was as if she were seeing her daughter and what she would have been at that age. Mama understood this, too, and often brought Katherine over there to play for an hour or two. If that could comfort Mrs. Latis, it was the least she could do.

*   *   *

Mrs. Latis never had any more children. There never was another little girl to replace the daughter she lost.

Katherine was daughter to two women now. She was the daughter of her own mama, where she rightfully belonged. And she was daughter to Mrs. Latis, in that lady's mind, anyway. She had become a substitute daughter.

Life was too busy for Katherine to be at the neighbor's house very often. But every so often, Mama would think about Mrs. Latis, feeling her continued pain. Then she would wipe her hands on a towel, prepare a plate of cookies or muffins, hand them to Katherine and say, "Child, will you take a walk and bring these to Mrs. Latis? You may play there one hour, okay?"

And Katherine would obediently walk the mile to the Latis' home. Always, Mrs. Latis seemed to know she was coming. She would meet her on the doorstep, waiting with a huge smile on her face. Always, Katherine received a hug and some sort of drink with a cookie, perhaps milk or maybe even tea or coffee, a real treat.

While Mama never allowed Katherine to drink coffee at home, she never said anything that Mrs. Latis allowed it. It wasn't that often, anyway. Just when there was nice weather and Mama thought of sending Katherine.

*   *   *

Mrs. Latis' attachment to Katherine never lessened as Katherine grew older and moved to the Yellow House. Often, Katherine would sit in church and feel Mrs. Latis' eyes on her.

Sometimes, if Mama thought to send Katherine over, she would take Dorothy along with her. Mrs. Latis never seemed to notice Dorothy, though. Her attention always focused on Katherine. But Katherine still felt better having her sister along.

Once Katherine graduated from school, Mrs. Latis began to feel a need for help. She would ask Mama if Katherine could come over and help for an afternoon. Maybe she needed help cleaning her cupboards. Or cleaning stovepipes. Perhaps butchering. Or making cheese. At least once a month she would request that Katherine help her. And Mama never refused.

Mama always felt pity. Such a tragedy!

If having Katherine there helped, why then, Katherine might go.

*　　*　　*

It was Dorothy who questioned the arrangement.

Dorothy hadn't yet been born when the tragedy occurred. She had heard the story but didn't remember the little girl. The impact on her was less great than it had been on Mama.

Dorothy thought it strange that Mrs. Latis had so attached herself to Katherine. She didn't accept it like Mama and Katherine had.

"You are not her little girl!" Dorothy would exclaim with irritation. "She has no right to think you have to help so often! It's time for her to get over it!"

Mama would shake her head, obviously still in pity for the woman. Katherine felt a bit uneasy but still thought Mrs. Latis was always nice to her. If it helped Mrs. Latis, what was the harm? Of course she missed her daughter; the accident had been awful! Katherine was okay with it if she could help her cope with the memory by going there once in awhile.

*　　*　　*

Without another daughter to help her forget, Mrs. Latis never did get over the grief.

She could only see Katherine occasionally. Between Katherine's visits, she moped.

Mrs. Latis' housework suffered. Mama said that she neglected her housework, seldom doing house cleaning, never washing windows, ignoring one thousand other little things.

That was depression, Papa said.

Depression of the mind. Depression of the mind meant that everything seemed dark and dismal, hopeless. Mrs. Latis didn't care about things anymore.

Except when Katherine went over. On those days, Mrs. Latis seemed to come to her senses. With Katherine there, she would be cheerful and bustle around, making a good meal and even cleaning things.

Since she was always nice to Katherine, and since her loss was so great, neither Mama nor Katherine ever said "No."

Mr. Latis was the neighborhood thresher. He would call meetings twice a year at his home. The first meeting was of all the farmers and their wives — children, too, were welcome — to plan the threshing. The second meeting was after threshing was finished. Then he would give every farmer the bills and everyone would make arrangements to pay for threshing.

Katherine always went along to these meetings. Sometimes the boys and Dorothy went, too, so it didn't feel strange. But always, Mrs. Latis would find a reason to come up to Katherine and talk to her. Always, she gave her a hug.

Even with Dorothy rolling her eyes, Katherine allowed it.

If that explosion had happened to Dorothy or to her, how would Mama have taken it?

No, Katherine was willing to help.

Even though Dorothy was right. It was strange.

Strange to be another mother's substitute daughter.

"... a man mine equal, my guide, and mine acquaintance. We took sweet counsel together ..."

Chapter 18. Thursday, December 4, 1946

Bloody Butchering

In just a few weeks, it would be Christmas.

There were so many things to do before Christmas! Pies to be baked. Good meat to be prepared. Food was always important.

To make pies, they needed lard. Since lard was fat from a hog, to get lard, they needed to butcher.

And in order to have good meat, they needed to butcher.

That large job had to be done in the cold weather before Christmas.

*   *   *

Willie and Katherine no longer attended school. Gerrit, Dorothy, and John left for school early in the morning. John had turned five in February so he was in kindergarten now; kindergarten had been added in recent years. Dorothy was responsible for him. Marvin was four years old, the only preschooler. Two out of school, three in school, one preschooler. Every year brought changes.

Hog butchering day was a day for adults to work together. It excluded school-aged children. Katherine sometimes worked like an adult with butchering. Other times, she was the babysitter who took care of Marvin.

Unlike hogs, turkeys or chickens could be butchered whenever there were a few extra hours. Sometimes they were killed the day they were eaten. Neighbors weren't needed to butcher chickens.

Butchering beef or pork, however, was a neighborhood affair. The Kroontjes butchered with Jake and Gertie Wulfsen, neighbors, and with Cornie and Fanny Tilstra, Mama's cousin and his wife, who lived a few farms away.

*   *   *

On a modern farm, if an animal is butchered, meat can be frozen.

Before electricity and freezers, things were different. Some methods of preserving meat were: (1) smoking; (2) dehydrating; (3) canning; (4) packing the meat in salt brine; (5) hanging the meat from rafters in the barn; or (6) packing the meat in containers in snow banks.

Papa and Mama never did smoking or salt brine or dehydrating. They either canned the meat or — after electricity arrived — brought it to a locker in town. Papa might "smoke" a few pieces of meat with a liquid smoke, brushing on the liquid to give it a smoked flavor. But it was preserved like other meat.

Most butchering was done after the weather turned cold.

In fact, most butchering was done after the first heavy snowfall.

*   *   *

In December of 1946, Katherine developed a bad "flu." She coughed and ran a fever. So Mama said she couldn't help with butchering.

Katherine, sixteen years old now, felt miserable with the fever but also felt guilty not helping. But Mama insisted she must not spread her illness.

Upstairs, Katherine took her pillow and blanket next to the stairway. Lying next to the open doorway, she could hear everything downstairs. The Wulfsens and the Tilstras were just arriving.

As everyone entered the house, Papa began the usual story-telling.

"My wife was helping a neighbor lady to butcher last week," said Papa as the men put on caps with ear flaps to go outside. Papa glanced over his shoulder to make sure Mama was listening. He loved to tease her.

"These neighbors hired a man to butcher for them, a *professional* butcher. He owned a tripod for hanging the hog, and had a fancy gadget for raising and lowering the hogs . . . everything up to snuff. Susie thought he'd have a fancy setup for killing the animal, too. So she decided to watch how he did it.

"Well, the man called to the hog, 'Here, Girlie, Girlie!'

" 'Nothing fancy about that,' thought my wife.

"But the ornery hog didn't move.

"So the man called again, 'Here, Girlie! Girlie!' and held out an ear of corn. Of course, any pig will head for an ear of corn, so the pig came running. The traveling butcher dropped the corn to the ground and the pig went right at it, eating the corn and forgetting the man.

"While the poor pig was mindlessly eating that ear of corn, the butcher raised a sledge hammer and . . . wham! Bam! Smashed that poor pig on the head.

"My wife is shocked. Vowed she'd stick with our old-fashioned methods of butchering. 'A well-jabbed knife was a lot more humane,' she thought.

"Only thing is," Papa added as the men stepped outdoors and out of earshot, "I really don't think the sledge hammer was more modern, do you? I think that guy was knife-shy and used the oldest butchering method on earth. That's probably left over from the cave man days before knives were invented!"

*　　　*　　　*

Katherine had watched the day before when Papa did the first step of butchering. Willie and Gerrit had helped with that.

They rounded up the hog they wanted to butcher. Papa had fed that pig a special diet for the past month. They each carried a large board so they could corral the hog and steer him out into the yard where they wanted him to be.

They wanted him right under a tree. In the tree they had already hung a "singletree" between branches. The singletree, a long piece of wood used to attach a harness to a plow, was the strongest piece of wood around. From it they could hang a pulley to raise the pig.

Katherine had long ago decided not to become friendly with pigs as they grew up. They were so cute when they were little that it would be easy to make a pig into a friend. However, it would be impossible to butcher a friend. So she ignored the pigs and let them just be . . . pigs. Meat. Bacon. Not friends.

This pig had balked. From the window upstairs, Katherine could see. He tried to run this way and that, squealing all the time like he was being butchered already. Since pigs squeal from birth, the boys were used to it.

The hog weighed over 300 pounds, Papa guessed. He didn't have a scale and couldn't know for sure. But he was fairly good at guessing weight.

Since Papa, Willie, and Gerrit had the pig safely within their three boards, he couldn't go anywhere and had to move with the boards. Soon the men had the pig below the tree with the singletree and pulley for his execution.

Willie and Gerrit, who were nearest the hog's rump, each grabbed onto a leg and held it securely. Papa quickly and expertly tied the hind legs together. Then he turned the crank of the pulley which lifted the pig into the air until it was dangling from its legs.

Katherine refused to watch. But she had heard the loud pig squeal.

*   *   *

The method for butchering which Papa used was (1) getting the hog into the air, tied by its hind legs, and (2) quickly slashing its throat.

It was almost painless. The pig was dead within seconds.

Katherine knew it was over as soon as the squeals stopped.

Although she didn't watch, Katherine knew the blood ran out onto the ground. The pig hung overnight so the blood was all out and the meat stiff.

Butchering was a bloody process.

*   *   *

But that was yesterday. The hog had hung overnight before the neighbors arrived today.

Papa had also sharpened tools needed for butchering. Hanging on nails inside the summer kitchen were three freshly sharpened saws. Lying on the butchering table were several sharpened knives — different sizes for different uses.

And Papa had done a third thing before the neighbors arrived. On butchering morning, he had set up a cauldron — a huge, black metal pot — below where the pig was hanging. He had piled corn cobs below the cauldron and gotten the cobs burning. Then he had filled the cauldron halfway up with water.

The first job the men had to do today was to take care of the hog's skin.

There were many uses for skin. But skin was useless unless they took care of it as they butchered. All the hair had to be scraped off — while still on the hog. Then the hair-free skin had to be cut off the hog.

To do this, the men would crank the pulley — still in place from yesterday — to lower the hog into the cauldron for a few minutes. They didn't want the hog in the cauldron too long or the meat would cook. The hog was in the hot water only until the skin was soft enough to scrape.

After the hog was dipped in the boiling water and raised back up again, the men would immediately start scraping the hair from the entire body. The men were efficient, so it didn't take long.

*   *   *

Next, using a sharpened saw, Papa and Mr. Smidstra carefully sliced the pig into two halves. As they cut, the intestines started sliding out . . . but the other men were ready with a large bowl to catch them. Even intestines had uses.

Cousin Cornie brought the bowl of intestines into the summer kitchen. The women squeezed out the innards and rinsed the intestines so the skins could be used to hold sausages. The skin of the innards were called *casings* because they were like cases to hold the sausage in place.

No part of the animal — *nothing* — went to waste.

Even the innards were given to animals for protein food.

*   *   *

Today, people cut off the head and discard it. It's embarrassing to think of eating anything from the head. It's *gross*, we think.

In Depression years, *nothing* went to waste. Nothing!

As Papa skillfully severed the head from the body, again the other two men stood with a bowl waiting to catch the head. It, too, was brought into the summerhouse. Mama already had a large pan of water cooking on the summerhouse stove. The head was lowered into the water where it cooked until all the meat was off the bones. Other meats would be added to it — the tongue, heart, liver, and kidneys (after they were flushed out) — and everything would be ground together, flour added, to form a meat spread called *head cheese*.

*   *   *

Katherine really felt sick. After watching the butchering process through the window for an hour, she crawled back to bed. Her cough was worse. She knew her forehead was hot.

But even as she closed her eyes, she knew what the men were doing.

Using saws, they were cutting the hog into sections.

Chops. Loins. Shoulders. Hams. Ribs. Bacon.

Even with her eyes closed, she knew what the women were doing.

The women cut excess fat off every piece of meat. They threw the fat pieces into a second large pan on the stove, where it cooked until the fat melted and everything that wasn't fat was floating in the fat.

The pure fat was called lard and everything else was called cracklings.

The women then poured the melted fat and cracklings through a "lard separator" — a big strainer. The fat, or lard, was melted liquid and ran through the holes. The cracklings stayed in the strainer.

The lard was put into containers to harden again. It was fat for cooking or making pies. Extra lard which might spoil before spring, Mama put into jars and canned. Mama made hundreds of pies using this lard — for Christmas and for every Sunday or special occasion.

Mama also made "worst." That was a Dutch word for sausage pressed into casings. The sausage was about an inch thick, made with special spices. Inside a two-quart jar, the long casings would be wound around and around. Papa sometimes teased Mama and called it "Mama's worst." Actually, it didn't mean "worst;" it meant "best," thought Katherine.

Mama would make *balkenbrij* from the cracklings.

Mama's "balkenbrij" was delicious. It was a way to use up cracklings instead of throwing them away. Mama mixed up cracklings, fat, flour, raisins if she had any, and salt. It had to be a good firm consistency. She pressed the mixture into loaf pans and hid them inside a snow bank to be preserved.

In the morning, Mama sliced the *balkenbrij* and fried it just as you fry eggs, on both sides, until lightly browned. Papa ate it like that. Katherine liked it the way Mama served it, with syrup spread over it like a pancake.

When she was eighty years old in a rest home, Katherine would still dream of Mama's *balkenbrij* and *worst*. To her, they were indeed Mama's *best*.

*   *   *

Katherine woke up to the sound of laughter in the kitchen below.

Her head felt better after the nap. Curious, Katherine again took her pillow to the top of the stairs. There she could hear every word in the kitchen.

All six of the men and women were taking a break from work. Mama had coffee on the stove and was serving applesauce cookies she had baked fresh yesterday. It smelled delicious.

This was the time to listen. Coffee time was story time.

*   *   *

"Good cookies, Susie!" Gertie Wulfsen said.

"May I have your recipe?" Fanny Tilstra agreed.

Katherine couldn't see Mama but could guess that she was blushing. Meanwhile, the men contentedly munched the cookies at the table.

"Butchering lasts from 7:00 to 7:00," Mr. Wulfsen said.

"Yeah, for three days," Cousin Cornie responded. "One day with all of us together, two days with the family alone."

"Well now, seven is an odd number, isn't it?" Mr. Wulfsen continued. "How can you turn the number seven into an even number?"

"Hmm-m-m . . ." thought Katherine. "Odd numbers are 1, 3, 5, 7, 9; even numbers are 0, 2, 4, 6, 8. How can an odd number become even?"

Cousin Cornie was figuring downstairs. "If you double the seven, you'll have fourteen. That's even, huh?"

But Papa figured out the correct solution.

"Take the 's' off 'seven' and you'll have 'even'. Aha!"

*   *   *

It was Cousin Cornie's turn to tell a joke.

"Did you hear about our neighbors who had half their hog stolen last week?" he asked. "They butchered on Wednesday and hung the hog up to cool overnight. On Thursday morning they went to get the hog to cut it up, and found only half the hog hanging there."

"Yeah," Mr. Wulfsen said, "I heard. It was stolen by a Democrat."

"No way!" replied Cousin Cornie. "Why do you say a Democrat stole it?"

"Because," responded Mr. Wulfsen, "he only took half. A Republican would have taken both halves."

Katherine heard Papa's laughter. She knew he'd be repeating that joke.

*   *   *

Right then Katherine heard the bottom landing of the stairway creak. Mama was coming upstairs to check on her!

Quickly she bolted back to bed. When Mama entered the room, she was lying under the blankets with her eyes closed.

Mama checked her forehead. "Katherine, how are you feeling?" she asked. "I have to go back into the summer house now. We have to get the meat into containers before it spoils. Would you like a glass of milk with a cookie?"

And Katherine, wishing she could join them in the summer kitchen, simply nodded meekly as she accepted the snack.

She had to agree with Gertie Wulfsen. The cookies were delicious!

Yes, she thought as she drifted back to sleep, *the best thing about butchering is the visiting. What can compare with friends and family who worship together on Sunday and help each other during the week?*

Katherine still today remembers that as a blessing of the Depression years. It is hard to find that kind of natural, delightful socializing in modern living.

"Oh . . . the days when God preserved me . . ."

Chapter 19. Fall 1947

Pop! Pop! Monday was Laundry Day!

Pop! Pop! Pop!

Katherine, in the barn milking the cows, heard the noise. Groaning, she whispered, "Oh, no. Mrs. Eihausen has beat us to it . . ."

It was Monday. On Mondays, every woman in the area did laundry. Laundry was the single most time-consuming and demanding job women had in those days. To get the laundry done in good order, a woman rose up long before the sun arose. Katherine had to help Mama but also had to milk the cows before she could help with laundry.

Most women had wash machines with gas motors. Electricity had not yet reached rural Iowa; gas machines were the best they could get. However, gas machines made a lot of noise. "Pop! Pop! Pop!" could be heard from a mile away. Every woman within a mile knew that laundry was being done.

Quickly finishing her last cow, Katherine grabbed the pails and cleaned up. While Willie finished cleanup in the barn, Katherine carried the milk into the summer kitchen. Gerrit would take care of the milk from here on because she had to help Mama with laundry.

*   *   *

The men had already been helping Mama. Papa and Willie hauled in water. As they brought water buckets into the kitchen, Mama poured the water into a large copper boiler on the stove to heat. The water had to be boiling hot to clean well and sterilize the clothes. Bleach wasn't used until a few years later. Boiling water took the place of modern bleach.

Once bleach became available, it was used mostly for white clothes. White clothes were bleached in hot water on the stove before they were put in the machine. Women liked how white the whites became with bleach.

As Katherine entered the kitchen, the first boiler of water had just begun to boil. A boiler was huge, too huge to carry alone. Together, Mama and Katherine took down the boiling boiler of water and carried it to the summer house. They poured it into the gas washing machine.

The engine of the washer was started with a pedal. On cold mornings, a pan of hot water would be placed under the machine to warm the oil so that it would start more easily. No fire or matches were used.

A few years later, an oil stove was put into the summer house so the water could be heated right there. But for now, Dorothy took the empty boiler back into the house for Mama to heat more water. Katherine pumped the pedal to ignite the gas for the washing machine. Soon their machine, too, made its merry "Pop! Pop! Pop!"

Now the neighbors knew that they, also, were washing laundry.

*   *   *

Washing lasted most of the day. First the delicates and whites had to be washed. Then school clothes. And last of all the farm clothes and towels. Water was reused as many times as possible to save the work of heating up too many boilers.

Mama used her own homemade soap. She would use Bon Ami on Saturdays for cleaning the nickel on the stove trim, the lamps, and other metals. But for laundry she used her own soap, made from pork lard mixed with lye. She would shave a bar of her lard soap until it became as fine as powder and would easily mix with boiling hot water. There had to be just enough soap in the water to get a fine layer of bubbles on top. Then clothes would get clean.

After the clothes swished about ten or fifteen minutes — longer for heavier clothes — Katherine used a heavy stick to take the clothes out of the boiling water. Very carefully, she started them through the wringer.

Then through the hot rinse water, in a metal tub next to the washer. After being again fished out and dripping for a minute, they went into cold rinse water. Then once more through the wringer. Then Katherine gave the clothes to Dorothy — if she was still home — to take into the house. In cold weather, they were hung on lines in the house to dry.

All the while, the washing machine continued its noisy "Pop! Pop!"

*   *   *

Right next to the washer in the summer house was an old window. It had cracked during the summer. Rather than replacing it right then, Papa taped it together to hold until he had time to buy new glass.

The lines in that broken glass radiated from the center outward to the edge of the wooden frame of the window. Right in the center, where the lines began, was a small hole. A windy draft sometimes entered through the hole.

Katherine mostly thought of that window as an eyesore. But she knew it would be fixed as soon as Papa had time and knew he was too busy in summer. That was a late fall job, after harvest but before it became freezing cold. Papa would fix any broken barn windows at the same time.

*   *   *

"The last batch!"

Katherine was pleased that the day was almost ended. Blissfully, she closed her eyes for one second. Meanwhile, she automatically reached with her stick for the last pair of jeans floating in the rinse water and jabbed it to start it through the wringer.

As the last pair of jeans squeezed out of the wringer, Katherine gave it the yank necessary to pull it out all the way. But suddenly, her hand slipped . . . and flew straight to the cracked window! Straight into the little hole in the center!

That glass was *sharp*! It cut her middle finger down to the bone. The finger bled profusely.

Katherine knew better than to head for the doctor. In those days one went to the doctor only for emergencies.

Rather, she ran into the house and asked Mama for scissors and an old pillowcase. Mama, seeing her wounded finger, left supper preparations and cut a pillowcase into strips. She wrapped one long strip tightly around the finger until the bleeding was staunched. Around it she wrapped another narrow strip of cloth and tied it on top to hold the long strip.

It was a good thing laundry was finished! That cut was indeed down to the bone and kept bleeding. Katherine couldn't work for the rest of that day. Dorothy, home from school now, had to take over her last jobs — using laundry water to scrub the sidewalks, the chamber pails, the outdoor toilet, and the summer kitchen floor.

By the next morning the finger had stopped bleeding and a single strip of cloth took care of it. That was good, because Papa and Mama had to go away.

There was again a pile of work . . . and Katherine was in charge.

"Be not overcome of evil, but overcome evil with good."

Chapter 20. Fall 1947. Part 2.

Sauerkraut and Gas Irons

"Katherine, if there is time . . ."

"Oh," moaned Katherine, "more work? I have enough to do!"

"If there is time," continued Mama, heading for the door, "then start doing the ironing, okay? Otherwise, we will start Wednesday with Tuesday's work and never catch up, right?"

"Yes, Mama," Katherine replied, outwardly meek . . . but inwardly rebelling. How would she get all the work done? Alone with Mama gone?

To Katherine, the work before her looked daunting, almost impossible. Especially with her finger still throbbing and bleeding.

*   *   *

Mama seldom left Katherine home alone. In fact, she seldom went away at all. Papa did most of the shopping in town. If Mama was gone, it was important.

Dorothy later tried to recall why Mama had been gone all day and Katherine home alone. It may have been because John, who was in second grade at that time, had two sets of teeth growing at the same time. His baby teeth were still in his mouth while his permanent teeth were pushing them out from underneath. A third set of teeth was pushing its way over the baby teeth. This had the unique result that it was drawing his eyes together, making him cross-eyed.

Once Papa and Mama both went with John to the dentist to get this third set of teeth pulled. Obviously, it was a traumatic day for John, and he needed both parents to comfort him.

Such events don't wait for perfect timing. The teeth didn't care that Katherine's hand was bleeding and a lot of work waiting at home. The dentist appointment was planned and had to happen . . . that day!

Later Dorothy teased John that he had stolen her second set of teeth — because she never got a second set for her lower teeth but kept her baby teeth. That is, she never knew she had the second set but it was there, all right, patiently waiting for the baby teeth to loosen and let them out. Dorothy finally got her second set of teeth in the 1970s, when she was about forty-five years old!

*   *   *

Wash on Monday,
Iron on Tuesday,
Patch on Wednesday,
Garden on Thursday,
Can on Friday,
Polish and Bake on Saturday.

Katherine's muttered schedule was not the familiar one of the nursery rhyme. She would gladly have traded hers for that!

The trouble was that Katherine's muttered schedule didn't tell half of the story. There were daily chores to be done, whether Monday or Tuesday or whatever day. Often Papa needed help with outdoor work. Gardening must be kept up with every day, not just on Thursday, and canning must be done whenever garden crops needed it, not only on Friday.

Before Mama had added the usual afternoon Tuesday ironing, she had said: "Katherine, cabbages are starting to break open. That means they are as large as they can get and if they grow anymore, they'll be spoiled.

"You must cut the biggest ones and shred them to make sauerkraut. That's a big job but it must be done. Can you get right at it?"

Making sauerkraut was a lot of work . . . and Katherine wasn't fond of the results. But it was a way to preserve and use the abundant cabbage. No food must be wasted. So Katherine nodded. Yes, she would shred the cabbage.

She hadn't rebelled about doing the cabbage — even with a half dozen heads to shred. Especially since John needed Mama today.

But, when shredding cabbage was a job that took hours, was it fair that she also had to do the ironing?

Katherine sighed. She knew Mama worked hard. It wasn't often that Mama had a day off. Even today, Mama had apologized that she couldn't be there to help. But it did seem sometimes like Katherine had to do *all* the work!

*   *   *

Sauerkraut was an old-time way of preserving cabbage. It was healthful, no doubt about that. Scientists say it may account for the long lives of old-time Germans and Dutchmen.

The first step in making sauerkraut was Katherine's first job this Tuesday afternoon. After bringing cabbage heads from the garden, she had to cut them in half, then in half again, then in half yet again, into eight wedges. She had to cut the center rind out of each wedge — eight times. And then she had to shred each wedge.

Katherine found six cabbages starting to split open.

Well, she might as well get at it. To start was the only way to finish!

When Papa cut cabbages in the field, his strong hands sliced them off in a few seconds. But Papa wasn't home. For Katherine, it was a struggle to cut those thick cabbage stems. It might take half a minute per cabbage. She had to be careful not to let the knife slip and cut her hand.

While still in the garden, she stripped off the thick outer leaves of the cabbage heads. Outside leaves had worm holes and rust spots, so were useless. By stripping them in the garden, she didn't have to throw them out later.

At least it wasn't hot outside. The first light snow had already fallen and Katherine was wearing a sweater. Gardening was worse when the sun was hot.

*   *   *

In the summer kitchen, Katherine chose the sharpest knives. Papa had already sharpened them on his large knife sharpener, driven by the tractor.

Then, chop! Katherine leaned with all her might on the knife to get it to cut through the cabbage — but she made it. The first cut was the hardest.

Chop. Chop. Chop . . . 48 difficult cuts, eight per cabbage. It was a relief to have the wedges cut.

Cleaning off the first knife, Katherine grabbed the thinner knife.

Off with the cores — 48 times. Cast them into the garbage.

Before Papa had bought a shredder, they had to cut each wedge about fourteen times to shred it. What a monotonous job!

But now, Katherine could take each of the 48 wedges and press it through the shredder. The shredder did the fine slicing for her. That saved time.

The shredder wasn't a machine. It was a sharp slicer nailed firmly onto a board. Katherine could swiftly slip a cabbage wedge through the shredder until the cabbage was finely cut into shreds.

Long before finishing, Katherine's fingers cramped up. She had to stop and stretch her fingers before continuing.

Her cut finger from the window didn't help. It was bleeding again, too.

*   *   *

At last shredding was finished. There was no clock in the summer kitchen but Katherine could tell by the sun that it was halfway through the afternoon.

As she had shredded cabbage, Katherine had scraped it into Mama's large crocks on the floor. Katherine now added salt to the crocks. The salt was a preservative. It also made the cabbage ferment so that every few days it needed to be rinsed off. Once the cabbage was fermented just enough, it must be canned. Then it would be good for eating whenever they needed it.

Making sauerkraut was a lot, lot, lot of work.

Too bad Katherine didn't like sauerkraut — even though it was so healthful.

*   *   *

From one distasteful job to another . . .

Having finished the cabbage, Katherine sighed but picked up the basket of men's Sunday shirts. With four brothers and a father, she had five Sunday shirts to iron. Not to mention Sunday dresses. The material was stiff and bulky, not like modern permanent-press which scarcely needs ironing. The best ironer did well to iron one of those miserable Sunday shirts in fifteen minutes.

"It's a good thing I love you, Papa," she whispered as she set up the ironing board and reached for the gas iron. This iron was supposed to be "state of the art." Katherine couldn't stand it because the gas fumes gave her headaches.

This iron had a round gas chamber above it to get it started quickly. In the body of the iron, where steam irons today have water, it had kerosene burning to keep the iron hot. Katherine poured a small amount of kerosene into the round chamber and lit it with a match. Meanwhile, she gradually added air to the kerosene to keep it from getting too hot. All the time she was ironing, Katherine would keep pumping in air so it wouldn't get too hot and burn the shirts.

As she began lighting the gas iron, Willie came into the summer kitchen. He grinned as he saw what Katherine was doing.

"Aha, that fun job, eh?" he teased. He knew she hated ironing.

"Yes, my least favorite of all my least favorite jobs," Katherine grumbled. She did not like the job nor did she like him teasing her about it!

"You should be grateful," Katherine continued. "At least you get to have a nicely pressed shirt on Sunday. Can't you say 'Thanks', huh?"

Just then the kerosene caught on fire. It had to catch fire, but this time, something went wrong. Instead of simply catching fire and burning the kerosene, the entire iron caught on fire. It instantly spread to the ironing board and that, too, caught on fire.

"Oh, my!" Katherine shrieked. That had never happened before. "What can I do? Willie, help . . ."

But Willie was right there and already in action.

Quick as a wink, he grabbed the burning board with the blazing iron still on it and simply threw both of them out into the freshly falling snow.

The falling snow put out the fire within seconds.

*   *   *

"Well, I guess that takes care of your favorite chore for today, right?" Willie now teased Katherine.

Even though she hated the job, Katherine was upset about the accident. She didn't know what she had done wrong but realized she had made some mistake. Besides that, she was feeling guilty about her bad attitude all day.

"Oh, Willie, what am I going to tell Mama?" she blurted out. She was sure Mama, though usually quiet spoken and gentle, would be upset.

"Don't worry, Katherine," Willie replied kindly. "I was right here and saw the whole thing. You weren't doing anything wrong that I could see. I will tell Mama what happened."

"Oh, Willie, thanks so much," Katherine replied. "Thanks, too, for putting out the fire for me. I don't think I would have dared to throw everything outside like you did. I would have gotten burned."

"You are welcome, my sister," Willie grinned at her. "I sort of do appreciate you ironing my Sunday shirts, you know.

"Think you'll get that iron fixed before Sunday?

"Think Mama will survive having you iron the shirts on a different day?"

His bantering lightened the mood. Katherine began to smile as well.

"I'm sure Mama would never let us go to church without our clothes being ironed!" she chuckled. "So maybe I'd better get out in that snow and rescue the iron. We'll have to see whether it can be salvaged."

"At least you got out of that chore for today," Willie teased her again. "I think you did it deliberately, Katherine. You know how you hate ironing."

"Think again, Big Brother," Katherine rejoined. "After all, what good would it do? I'll still have to do it later, right?

"But," she then had to admit, "I am awfully glad that I don't have to do it right now. I'm already tired from shredding the cabbage. And my hand is still bleeding from yesterday's accident. Maybe tomorrow I can do the ironing right after dinner, when I'm not so tired."

"And now you can get at making supper," Willie grinned. He was always hungry . . . and rubbed his stomach in anticipation.

"Yes, come to think of it, it did turn out for the best," Katherine chuckled. "But don't you dare repeat that to Mama!"

The Magnolia Farmhouse, 1948

The Magnolia Farm, 1948

Chapter 21. February, 1948

Farewell, Little Yellow House

"Susie and Katherine! Would you like a car ride?"

Papa's big voice boomed through the house, where Katherine and Mama were finishing breakfast dishes. Looking up in surprise, Katherine saw a smile stretching across Papa's face from ear to ear.

What? Why would Papa want them to stop work to take a ride?

"Why, Wilbur?" asked Mama, "where are we going? I have a lot of work to get done. There is company coming on Sunday and . . ."

"I'll explain as we go. That could take an extra ten minutes, more if you ask questions. Just grab a coat and come along, okay? You'll be glad you did. I want your advice."

Although bursting with curiosity, they didn't ask questions. They put on their coats and headed for the car.

* * *

Papa's Ford Deluxe, bought in 1941, was green, a color Papa liked. He had seen an ad which read, "There's a FORD in your future!" and he agreed. Their family had gotten so squashed in the Model A Ford that they couldn't get to church without all their clothes being wrinkled.

The Ford Deluxe was no longer new but still rode well. Today, Papa and Mama sat in the front seat, just the two of them. In the back seat, 19-

year-old Willie sat by the left window and 17-year-old Katherine by the right window, just the two of them. Lots of room!

Gerrit, Dorothy, John, and Marvin were in school. None of them were on the ride.

Imagine! Letting work sit idle while they went for a ride!

What did Papa have planned?

* * *

Katherine was even more surprised when she saw the direction Papa was driving. He was not heading south and west towards Rock Rapids. He drove one mile west to get onto a better road, then north to the newly tarred Highway 90, and then east. Where on earth were they going?

But as he drove, Papa began to explain.

"Katherine, would you object to having a full closet in your bedroom?"

Perplexed, Katherine replied, "Of course not, Papa. Right now I have only a short clothesline for clothes. But you know there's no room . . ."

"Willie!" Papa called to the seat behind him. "John and Marvin sleep in the girls' bedroom right now, a curtain dividing the room. You and Gerrit share the boys' bed. How would you like to have a boys' room for all four of you, two full-sized beds, sleeping two to a bed?"

"Yeah, right!" groaned Willie, who was full grown and crowded in the small bed he had been sharing with Gerrit. "And how do you plan to do that? Throw all my radio equipment into the snow?"

"Well . . ." Papa began . . .

But suddenly the light dawned. "O-ho, Papa!" Katherine interrupted. "Are we going to look at a house? A larger house?"

Papa's laugh bounced through the car.

"Good for you, Katherine! You guessed first!

"You both know that your mother and I have been looking for a larger farm and house for several years. It was difficult to find one.

"Well, this morning Mr. Dykhouse, the real estate agent from Rock Rapids, stopped me and told me about a farm that just this week went for rent near Magnolia in Minnesota. Mr. Dykhouse hasn't seen it himself but said it sounded like it might fit our needs.

"I figured we might as well look at it together and check out possibilities. Mr. Dykhouse will lead the way and show us the place.

"Remember, we might not like it. Or it might be too expensive. But at least we'll have the fun of looking together.

"I'm *hoping* it will be the farm we're needing.

"And if we like it, we'll be seeing it before it's even advertised!"

*   *   *

Magnolia was a thirty minute drive from the Little Yellow House.

Papa pointed out that they were following the car of Mr. Dykhouse, the real estate agent. The owner of the farm, Mr. Ross, lived in California. He would fly back to check things but the real estate agent had to find a renter.

They drove east through Magnolia, then two miles north, and then another half mile east. There they spied a neat lawn with lots of trees shading a large house in the background. The real estate agent turned into its driveway.

"This must be it," Papa said gravely. "Be respectful, Children. Mama and I will do the talking, okay? You are only to look. I'll ask your opinion later."

Wilbur and Katherine were delighted just to be able to "look." They were amazed at the neatly trimmed yard with all the well-placed trees. The house in the background looked like a palace compared to the dinky yellow house in Iowa. To think they'd lived there seven years already!

Papa and Mama walked first. Katherine and Willie lagged behind.

Katherine couldn't hear the conversation between Papa and Mr. Dykhouse. Besides, she was too busy looking to listen.

What a house! Could they afford to rent a farm with such a fine house?

And that barn — why, it was HUGE! It could house double the animals of the barn they now had! That hay mow could hold double the hay, too. Katherine cringed a little at the thought of having to harvest twice as many crops as they already did. Surely Papa would hire more help?

And . . . look! A silo! Farms were just starting to have silos.

Plus . . . could it be? Was that an electric pole in the yard? Could this house possibly have electricity?

What a fine place to live! Katherine hardly dared hope it could happen. She was sure it would cost too much and be impossible to afford.

But wouldn't it be wonderful? It didn't hurt to dream, did it?

*   *   *

The closer they came to the house, the more Katherine gawked.

Look at all those windows! All sparkling clean — and so many!

Mr. Dykhouse unlocked the door and waited while the four of them approached the front of the house. Later there would be an enclosed porch here, but not yet. Mr. Dykhouse held the door open so they could enter the house.

Just as in both House 1 and House 2, the porch door opened into the kitchen. "Mr. Kroontje," said Mr. Dykhouse grandly as he flicked on a light switch near the doorway, "this kitchen is spacious enough to eat in every day, even with your fine family. You can see there are plenty of cupboards and room for your own cupboards, too. Off to the side is a large pantry. You can keep sugar and flour bins in here."

"And," thought Katherine, "there will be electric light for cooking!"

Mr. Dykhouse led them to the dining room. Before entering it, he stopped to point out a large cupboard. Since it was empty of dishes, he suggested they lean inside to look. They could see right through the cupboard into the dining room! Katherine thought that was marvelous — dry and put away dishes from the kitchen side, take them out in the dining room.

Now they entered the large dining room. Mr. Dykhouse pointed out that since they could eat daily meals in the kitchen, this room could be kept clean for unexpected company.

"And," mused Katherine, "we won't need kerosene lanterns for light!"

Two more rooms opened off the dining room.

To one side was the master bedroom. While smaller than the dining room, it was easily double the size of the bedroom Papa and Mama now had. Glancing at Mama, Katherine could see hope shining in her eyes.

To the other side was a room which now had no furniture but Mr. Dykhouse announced it to be a living room. Some people called it a parlor. "This is a room to visit with company," he explained proudly. "You can keep it clean all the time so you can visit in style even when unexpected guests arrive."

Imagine, two whole rooms always clean for company! Why, this was the lap of luxury!

Katherine saw Papa glance at Mama. They both saw stars in her eyes. She could hardly imagine having this much space for living — plus electricity.

*   *   *

"Now let's go upstairs. Here are the stairs, next to the living room."

Katherine noticed a door to the outside right by the stairs. If company came they could run upstairs first to change clothes before they were seen, and then come down to meet the guests.

Leaping up the sturdy wooden stairs, Mr. Dykhouse waited at the top. Papa and Willie also leaped up two steps at a time. Mama and Katherine walked up more sedately.

Everyone found themselves in an upstairs hallway. This was a *real* upstairs, not an attic! From the stairs, they turned left into a hallway. Two doors — real doors, not curtains! — were on the right side, and one door on the left side. All three doors had shiny brass doorknobs. Before she even saw the rooms, Katherine knew this was an improvement over their tiny upstairs in Iowa.

And a flick of a light switch flooded the dim hallway with light.

The doors on the right opened into two nice-sized bedrooms. Mama promptly decided that — if they rented this farm — the smaller of these rooms would be for her hired girl, the larger room for Katherine and Dorothy.

Opening the door on the left side of the hallway, they found a huge room stretching all the way across the upstairs. It had plenty of space for all four boys to sleep with comfort. If the boys wanted, Mama could place a curtain down the middle so the boys would have two separate bedrooms.

And those bedrooms had light switches, too!

It was a good thing Papa had told the children not to say anything. Katherine had all she could do not to beg him to rent the place. How grand to have such space! To have electricity besides! It seemed an impossible dream.

*   *   *

While Papa stayed behind to check the other buildings and to talk finances with Mr. Dykhouse, Mama and the children returned to the car.

"Willie, do you think we'll move here?" Katherine was wide-eyed with wonder. She couldn't imagine renting such a farm.

Mama squeezed Katherine's hand gently.

"Patience, my dear. We must wait," she replied softly. "That's what Papa is talking about with Mr. Dykhouse. But isn't it a nice place?"

Katherine nodded. It was too much to imagine.

Mama's eyes never strayed from Papa and the real estate agent. Though she said nothing more, her eyes said everything. Katherine could feel Mama's longing. For nineteen years Mama had lived with hardly any room to move around. How wonderful this would be!

*   *   *

At last Papa headed toward the car. The smile on his face and the twinkle in his eyes told everyone the results long before he started the car and left the yard. Katherine's stomach quivered in expectation.

"Well, Children," Papa said as they cruised away from the farm and back towards the Little Yellow House, "are you ready to begin packing?"

That ended the silence. Whoops and cheers filled the small Ford.

Mama never said a word but stared straight ahead. Wondering, Katherine leaned over to look. She was startled to see tears running down Mama's face.

As Papa reached over and took Mama's hand, Katherine understood. These were tears of joy. Mama had lived in tiny houses for so long that she could hardly believe things would finally improve.

* * *

This was the first home they would have with *electricity*. It had just been installed in rural Minnesota after World War II ended. Not all homes had it yet.

There was still *no telephone* although that was installed soon after moving.

There was still *no indoor plumbing*. That, too, reached the Midwest later. The house still had chamber pots and an outhouse.

But what an improvement! The family had been cramped for so long they could hardly believe the wonderful improvements.

* * *

At supper, Papa told Gerrit, Dorothy, John, and Marvin about the new farm they had looked at . . . and were intending to rent.

"We must remember," he said solemnly, "that happiness does not lie in things. God made us happy as a family living here in this tiny house, hasn't He?

"Where do we find true happiness, Dorothy?" he quizzed her.

Dorothy had just memorized the first question and answer of the *Heidelberg Catechism*. She was able to quote that precious answer: *"That I, with body and soul, in life and death, am not my own but belong unto my faithful Savior, Jesus Christ."*

"Amen!" Papa responded, his eyes glistening as he listened to that beloved response. "Always treasure that, my children. Nothing in this life is as important as belonging to the Savior.

"We needed a larger home. We are thankful God is providing it. But let's always put first the things of the Kingdom and God's righteousness. Then He will add earthly things as we need them.

"Shall we thank Him for all His provisions? For the years we've had in this Little Yellow House? For our memories?

"Let's ask Him to lead us as we move from this house into a new state, a new home, new schools, and a new church. He is our God in Rock Rapids and will continue to be our God in Magnolia. He has been faithful in the past and will lead us also in the future."

Mama and all the children joined Papa in bowing their heads. Then Papa prayed: "We thank Thee, Father, for Thy faithfulness . . ."

Postlude #1

In Memoriam

On Thursday, December 29, 2011, I found a parcel in the mailbox. What a parcel! The first proof had arrived of *Book 1: Little White Farmhouse in Iowa.*

I couldn't wait to show Katherine . . . impossible anymore that day. But I gift-bagged the book to bring to her on Friday, the following day.

Katherine never saw that book.

On Friday morning, I returned a cell phone call from Dorothy. Imagine my shock to hear that Katherine had passed away. On Wednesday, she had been unable to breathe. Measures to solve this failed. It was God's time for Katherine to go Home.

Instead of taking the book to Katherine, I gave it to Dorothy. Although Katherine never saw the book, at her funeral it was placed on a memoirs' table to represent her life — not only her childhood, which it was about, but her last three years, during which she had worked so hard to bring these books into existence.

I am thankful the first book was there for family and friends to see! Many now own it, a lasting testimony to her life.

Katherine was continually conscious of her weak health. As a result, I promised her many times that, if she passed away from this life, I would continue the work to make sure her siblings and children received copies of all three finished books.

It is a promise I am attempting to keep. The first drafts of Books 2 and 3 were already written while Katherine was alive. Dorothy is assisting me in proofing for accuracy. Our hope is that on the anniversary of Katherine's entrance into heaven, her three books will all be in existence on earth.

As we so often said together: "If God wills . . . If God wills . . ."

Carol Brands, friend of Katherine

Postlude #2

by Dorothy Kroontje Ricehill

Remembering Katherine

Losing my sister created an empty place in my life. The schedule no longer holds "time with Katherine." A thought is not completed: "I wonder if Katherine would enjoy . . ." And, as soon as I think this, I feel that emptiness that says, "No, she is not here any longer."

What I have are the lovely things she crocheted for me, gifts she gave me, and precious memories of her hospitality. She baked the *best* pies and homemade bread. Her flower gardens were special and she gave me many lovely bouquets. She was a terrific sister and friend. Now it has all become a part of my memories.

Today, my brothers — Gerrit, John, and Marvin — and I are trying to fill in the gaps in Carol's "Katherine Stories." The basic outlines were completed before Katherine's Home-going — but filling in details or clarifying facts has become our part in books two and three.

We appreciate all the time Carol has given to these books. She has helped us remember our childhood and has given our children and grandchildren a realistic peek into the life we lived. We hope the people who read these books will gain some understanding of what life was like during those years.

Dorothy Kroontje Ricehill

Postlude #3

For the Historical Record

We were pleased with the many comments we received concerning this postlude in Book 1. We are therefore making sure to also include it in Books 2 and 3. For all readers who want to know how reliable this book is as a biography, this is for you.

Chapter 1. Dorothy doesn't recall the house being in such bad shape as did Katherine. Also, Dorothy says they never called the upstairs an attic; if "attics" were lived in, they were simply called the upstairs.

Chapters 2. Couldn't find anything not factual here!

Chapter 3. These three events happened as told; only the narrative has been invented.

Chapters 4 - 5. Fixing up the yellow house happened much like it was narrated. The episode with Katherine's mishap is authentic.

Chapter 6. All accurate except for the snowball bantering of the children.

Chapter 7. All information and remarks about recesses are accurate.

Chapter 8. All information about piano lessons and music is authentic.

Chapter 9. All accurate — the dresses, the testing, graduation information . . . except Papa never called Katherine "princess."

Chapter 10. The information in this chapter is from Gerrit, not Katherine. Thanks, Gerrit!

Chapter 11. Only the narrative is fictional. All the facts about the childrens' fun and perms is accurate.

Chapter 12. Dorothy remembers several details differently. (1) The date was inaccurate — it actually happened in the Little White House, when she was only five years old. (2) The neighbor boys weren't *always* teasing; often they played well together. (3) Since these neighbor boys lived in the Little Yellow House, it was after they moved away that the Kroontjes moved into that same house. So this must have happened in 1940.

Chapter 13. Gerrit did collect matchbooks and knew a lot about them, but his essay is fictional, inserted for historical background. The fire was real.

Chapter 14. Daily chores' description and details about "Katherine's worst memory" are as accurate as we could make them.

Chapter 15. The hen house sliver details are as accurate as the memory would allow.

Chapter 16. The entire episode of corn picking and runaway horses is authentic memory.

Chapter 17. The name "Latis" is invented to protect the real family's identity. The explosion and fire, as well as Katherine's "adoption" by the depressed lady, is real.

Chapter 18. The jokes told during butchering are samples of real jokes told back then but were not necessarily told that butchering day. Facts about the butchering day are accurate — except, we aren't sure if the Kroontjes made "head cheese." Perhaps this was the Brands! Also, we aren't sure what Katherine's "illness" was — it might have been female related.

Chapter 19. Dorothy believes neighbors were too far apart in Iowa to hear each other's "Pop! Pop!" This idea was the author's from her mother's stories of Illinois, where neighbors lived closer together — and Katherine agreed with it, but may have just consented to please the author. The rest of the story is authentic.

Chapter 20. The bantering is fictional. The rest of the story is biographical.

Chapter 21. Finding the third home in Minnesota did happen through Mr. Dykhouse, the Rock Rapids' Real Estate Agent, as described.

Most of the book's emotions, devotions, and conversations are fictional, to make the story flow. Family memorabilia are inserted wherever it fits, not in chronological importance.

Postlude #4

Uncle Bill's Navy Experiences

January 7, 1941 through December, 1944.
For family and anyone else who is interested!

Official World War II Muster Records for William Tilstra

2-28-42	USS WHITNEY Seaman 2c, V-6
3-17-42	USS BLUE Seaman 2c, V-6
4-30-42	Seaman 2c, V-6
6-30-42	USS BLUE F3c, M1c V-6 USNR
7-9-42	USS BLUE F3c Sailed from Sydney, Australia
9-2-42	USS ZEILIN (USS BLUE) *F2c From Espiritu Santos Island to Sea
9-11-42	USS ZEILIN F2c From White Poppy to Long Bow
9-30-42	USS PATTERSON F2c, V-6 Received 9-28-42
11-30-42	USS ZEILIN F2c White Poppy to Long Bow
12-10-42	USS PATTERSON F2c, V-6
12-31-42	USS PATTERSON *F1c, V-6
3-31-43	USS PATTERSON F1c, V-6 Received 9-28-42
6-30-43	USS PATTERSON F1c, V-6 Received 9-28-42
7-4-43	dos USS PATTERSON Flc, V-6 —— to ———
7-30-43	USS PATTERSON F1c, V-6 Received 9-28-42
9-30-43	USS PATTERSON *M2c, V-6 Received 9-28-42
11-30-43	dos USS PATTERSON M2c, V-6

It took three hours of research and $70.76 to access a naval site in order to obtain the above information. It was worth it! We finally have an official history of the ships on which Uncle Bill was registered during World War II.

We'll use the above record along with family memories to build a snapshot photo of what Uncle Bill endured during the war. The muster records need interpretation by family records.

The ships' muster records of Bill Tilstra all recorded that his enlistment date was December 31, 1941. His enlistment also is recorded as being in Des Moines, Iowa. However, the family insists — supported by registration papers — that he arrived in Pearl Harbor on December 6. He never had boot camp but, as he said, "hit the ground running." So the picture becomes this:

Uncle Bill — who had considered enlisting in the war already on Memorial Day of 1941, didn't actually enter the war until shortly before Pearl Harbor. He enlisted in Des Moines, Iowa, from where he was immediately sent to California via train and then to Hawaii via a "potato boat." He was officially assigned to the *USS Arizona* but its muster records were lost when it sank. Besides that, he never actually set foot on the *Arizona*. On the morning of December 7, Uncle Bill went to church on land intending after church to locate and join his assigned ship, the *Arizona*. Instead, coming out of church he witnessed from land the demolition of the fleet in Pearl Harbor. Thus, his first assigned ship was destroyed.

The *Whitney* is the first official ship showing "William Tilstra" on its "muster log." Since none of the family recalls this name, the *Whitney* must have been a ship which was temporary in Uncle Bill's assignment of cleaning up the harbor. Most likely the *Whitney* took Uncle Bill to his first transport ship, the *Yorktown*, getting him to it in early June.

The family maintains that Uncle Bill was on the *USS Yorktown* for two or three weeks. The *Yorktown* was a sizable aircraft carrier. Since no muster records show him on this ship, I draw this conclusion: he wasn't *listed* on the *Yorktown* since for him it was a *transport* ship to the *USS Blue*. After all, he is mentioned on the muster records of the *USS Blue* in March and April, although he didn't actually set foot on it until June.

Uncle Bill was still on the *Yorktown* when it was torpedoed in June of 1942. After hours of floating in the ocean, he was picked up by the *HMAS Canberra* and transferred to the *USS Blue*. Thus, his second important — though only transport — ship was destroyed.

From March 17, 1942, through September, 1942, Uncle Bill officially served on the *USS Blue*. He was officially a "Seaman Second Class" (S2C) in March and April, while still on the *Whitney* en route to the Yorktown. Within three months he had enough training to become a Fireman Third Class (F3C), still officially a "U.S. Naval Recruit." But on June 30, after the *Yorktown*'s demise, he was classified M1c which means he had a medical disability, not so severe he couldn't stay aboard ship. This is the first of his three medical injuries, each one worse.

By July 9, when the *USS Blue* sailed from Sydney, Australia, into the war of Solomon's Sea with all its islands, Uncle Bill was serving in the boiler room. Near the end of August, the *USS Blue* had an encounter with the Japanese which destroyed the ship.

Family information says that the *USS Blue* was attacked by a Kamikaze, a Japanese suicide bomber. The pilots knew they would die because they would dive straight into a target ship to make it explode and sink. The attack is a marvelous story of God's preservation since Uncle Bill was called up to the deck by a loudspeaker message only seconds before the Kamikaze attack. The airplane hit the boiler room in which he had been working with buddies and thus Uncle Bill escaped a brutal death by scalding water even though he suffered the trauma of knowing how his buddies had died. Now, a third ship — second assigned — was destroyed.

At this time Uncle Bill's second medical injury occurred. To escape the sinking *USS Blue,* he had to jump from the Blue's deck into a small boat with interlaced wooden slats. The men sat with their feet in the water. The jump dislocated Uncle Bill's ankle. It swelled and was very painful during his twenty-four hours in the water and for over a month following that, even after it was in a cast.

Uncle Bill spent twenty-four hours in the ocean before landing on the Espiritu Santos Island. Two weeks later the *USS Zeilin* — according to muster records — rescued him and others of the *USS Blue.* According to family records and local newspapers, however, he was rescued by the USS *Helm.* It is not clear why there is a discrepancy in the name of the rescuing ship.

What is interesting is that God used this rescue to strengthen him by a most unusual reunion aboard ship. Bill had joined the war effort in December, before Pearl Harbor. Two of his back-home farm neighbor friends — the Millinex brothers, Howard and Robert — had joined a month later, in January, following Pearl Harbor. The ship on which the neighbor boys served was used to rescue him. Home papers were quite excited about this unusual overseas reunion.

There is also a story about the ship — family tradition calls it the *Helm* — being torpedoed in its side and needing repairs. Checking the muster records, it appears that this did not happen immediately. Uncle Bill was officially transferred to the *USS Patterson* after his first rescue and was on it for two months. Then records show that for ten days, for some unexplained reason, he returned to his rescue ship, which it calls the *Zeilin.* It is most likely that when Uncle Bill saw that his friends' ship had been torpedoed and he was asked to help, he returned for ten days to that ship in order to make emergency repairs while the ship limped to land for permanent repairs. This not only helped his neighbor friends to survive but also gave them another ten days together. This reunion was God's hand to strengthen him so far from home and alone.

There is no doubt that an interesting anecdote here is genuine. When Uncle Bill jumped from the *USS Blue*, he dislocated his leg. When rescued, the rescuing ship had a doctor aboard who put the leg back into place and put a cast on the ankle. When Uncle Bill went under water to weld his friends' torpedoed ship, he did the welding with the cast still on his leg. That made his volunteer help doubly heroic.

Another interesting anecdote occured about this time — which demonstrates both Dutch thriftiness and family concern. Uncle Bill was issued a new pair of navy boots every six months. Since he took good care of them, he did not need the new pair and knew that his father back home could use them. So every six months he sent a new pair of boots back home to his father. These must have lasted some years!

The muster records show Uncle Bill on the *USS Zeilin* (*Helm*) for 19 days. During this time he was promoted to "Fireman Second Class" (F2C) before being transferred on September 28 to the *USS Patterson*, which became his main ship until the end of his service. Doubtless this promotion was due to the *USS Blue* disaster. A month after his second time on the *USS Zeilin*, he was promoted to Fireman First Class (F1C), an unusual promotion within a year of service. This was most likely due to his heroic work of welding the *Zeilin/Helm*.

At all events, by September 10, 1942, Uncle Bill was back on the *USS Patterson* and remained on it until August, 1943 (officially until November 30, 1943).

The *USS Patterson*'s problems on September 22 were serious but did not destroy the ship. It had two problems during that night. First, it was torpedoed, which caused loss of control of the ship. Second, loss of control caused the ship to ram into another ship. When the two ships collided, the bow of the *Patterson* was severed. The *Patterson* was able to be fixed and continued in the war.

Uncle Bill, however, was seriously injured in the attack. He was in the engine or boiler department, where he worked on every ship he was on. His injuries were severe. He had shrapnel in his hands and kidneys and all over his body.

Fellow sailors joked that Uncle Bill was a "jinks" because every ship to which he was assigned sank! That was true of the *Yorktown* and the *Blue* but not of the *Patterson*. Since in all three cases Uncle Bill survived, however, we see God's hand of blessing.

As noted above, at the end of 1942, he was promoted to "Fireman First Class" (F1C). He maintained that status until he became M2C for two months and then MC1 — doubtless meaning that he was "Medical 2nd Class, still being treated, and then "Medical First Class," heading back home for treatment. It is interesting that 11-30-1943 was the "date of sailing" of the *USS Patterson* and Uncle Bill was still on its official rostrum even though he was being medically treated in Australia.

In January of 1944, following his injury, Uncle Bill was sent back to the United States to the Virginia Naval Medical Center, Portsmouth, Virgina. Here the last stages of his romance and marriage occurred.

Bill first met Maxine Saunders, his future wife, before he was in the service. She was born and raised in Beresford, South Dakota. She had moved to Inwood, Iowa, to teach. While a teacher, she had a flat tire alongside a country road. Bill came along and was able to help. This led to a few dates before he entered the service and to writing letters while he was in the service. Bill, who was very homesick, wrote the first letter. When Bill's ship was able to dock in Chicago, she was able to meet his ship and visited him there. He had also dated her while home on furlough.

When Uncle Bill headed for the Virginia Naval Medical Center, he immediately wrote Maxine. She dropped everything to head for Virginia. By then they were unquestionably in love so Uncle Bill asked her to marry him and she agreed. No family members could possibly drive out there so they were married by a justice of the peace, on December 28, 1944, while Uncle Bill was still in and out of the hospital. Maxine wore a simple blue suit. The Justice of the Peace was a very matter of fact man. The family still laughs how he married them: "I now pronounce you man and wife . . . and that will be $2.00."

Uncle Bill had been in treatment for over fifteen months when they married. A newspaper account says he returned to the United States in January of 1944 and had a medical discharge in October of 1944, although he was still in treatment when they married in December. Their first residence near the Virginia hospital is unknown but after they moved to Minneapolis, their residence was 4934 Girard Avenue S, Minneapolis, Hennepin, MN 55419.

Wedding photo of Uncle Bill and Aunt Maxine

Postlude #5

Credit Where Credit is Due

Chapter 1. "Home, Home, Sweet, Sweet Home" is credited to John Howard Payne, written when he was abroad.

Chapter 2. Deuteronomy 31:6: "Be strong and of a good courage . . . for the Lord thy God, He it is that doth go with thee; He will not fail thee, nor forsake thee."

Chapter 3. "The clouds ye so much dread are big with mercy, and shall break in blessings on your head." William Cowper, 1800s.

Chapter 4. Proverbs 31:17: "a virtuous woman . . . strengtheneth her arms."

Chapter 5. Proverbs 17:22: "A merry heart doeth good like a medicine."

Chapter 6. Psalm 25:2: "O my God, I trust in Thee: let me not be ashamed, let not mine enemies triumph over me."

Chapter 7. Proverbs 20:11: "Even a child is known by his doings, whether they be good or whether they be evil."

Chapter 8. Psalm 33:2-3: "Praise the Lord with the harp: Sing unto Him with the psaltery and an instrument of ten strings. Sing unto Him a new song; Play skilfully with a loud noise."

Chapter 9. II Timothy 2:15: "Study to shew thyself approved unto God, a workman that needeth not to be ashamed."

Chapter 10. Romans 8:26: "The Spirit also helpeth our infirmities; for we know not what to pray for as we ought; but the Spirit maketh intercession for us with groanings that cannot be uttered."

Chapter 11. Ecclesiastes 1:2, 12:8: "Vanity of vanities, saith the Preacher, all is vanity."

Chapter 12. Proverbs 17:17: "A friend loveth at all times, and a brother is born for adversity."

Chapter 13. James 3:5b: "Behold, how great a matter a little fire kindleth!"

Chapter 14. I John 2:10a: "He that loveth his brother abideth in the light."

Chapter 15. Proverbs 27:6a: "Faithful are the wounds of a friend."

Chapter 16. Ecclesiastes 2:24: "There is nothing better for a man, than that he should eat and drink, and that he should make his soul enjoy good in his labor."

Chapter 17. Job 1:21b: "The LORD gave, and the LORD hath taken away; blessed be the name of the LORD."

Chapter 18. Psalm 55:13-14: ". . . it was thou, a man mine equal, my guide, and mine acquaintance. We took sweet counsel together . . ."

Chapter 19. Psalm 16:1a. "Preserve me, O God, for in Thee do I put my trust."

Chapter 20. Romans 12:21: "Be not overcome of evil, but overcome evil with good."

Chapter 21. "*Great is thy Faithfulness, Lord, unto me*" is the conclusion of the song by Thomas O. Chisholm.

—All Bible quotations are from the King James Version.—

Postlude #6

Glossary of Names

Which Names Do You Recognize?

At the suggestion of Lori Ehde, editor of the *Luverne Star-Herald* and niece of Katherine, we added this postscript section to each of our books. Here, in alphabetical order, are listed names of people mentioned in this book. Whom do *you* know? Are *your* grandparents in it?

Strangers in Minnesota

"I am a stranger here, within a foreign land,
My home is far away, upon a golden strand."

Tears filled Katherine's eyes as she sang the song. Had God known how she felt? Had He given her this song, today, of all days?

She knew the song was not meant to describe moving from place to place on earth. It wouldn't even describe her grandparents, who moved from Holland to America. The song meant being strangers on earth. Our real Home is heaven.

But this was exactly how she felt — like a stranger in a strange land!

Everything seemed foreign. She was in a new state: not Iowa anymore, but Minnesota. She had a new home: not Rock Rapids, her home for nearly eighteen years, but Magnolia. She had left behind all her familiar friends — no friends or even acquaintances out here. She knew no one!

Now, she was even in a new church. Indeed: a stranger in a strange land!

"Father," she whispered, "help me to find friends here in Minnesota."

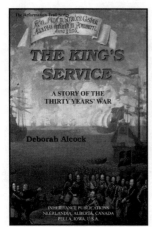

The King's Service
by Deborah Alcock
A Story of the Thirty Years' War

Once again Deborah Alcock has delicately woven together an accurate historical novel. This book gives wonderful insights into some of the events surrounding the thirty-years-war in which Gustavus Adolphus of Sweden gives his life for the Protestant cause. But even amidst the ravages of war life continues to weave its story of intrigue, romance, loyalty, and treason.

Two motherless children, Jeanie and Hugh, have been in the care of their Uncle Charlie ever since their father left about eight years earlier to fight for the Protestant cause. Uncle Charlie, a restless bachelor, subsequently leaves the bulk of Jeanie and Hugh's upbringing to the Presbyterian minister. He faithfully teaches these orphaned children the beautiful tenants of the Reformed faith. But when Uncle Charlie decides to leave his beloved Scotland to join the army of Gustavus Adolphus in Germany, Hugh wants to go along. Jeanie will go along as companion to Captain Stuart's wife and meets Fraulein Gertrud von Savelburg in Germany. Sifting through the reports and rumours of the times she comes to some disturbing and perplexing conclusions. What has made Uncle Charlie so sad, and why does a Roman Catholic priest regularly visit Hugh?

Time: 1630-1632   Age: 12-99
ISBN 978-1-894666-06-0   Can.$11.95 U.S.$11.95

How Sleep the Brave by James H. Hunter
A Novel of 17th Century Scotland

"Hush ye, hush ye, little pet ye,
Hush ye, hush ye, do not fret ye,
The Black Avenger shall not get ye."

Even though the Scottish covenanters endured harsh persecutions by the King's Inquisition the mysterious name of the Black Avenger sent thrills of hope and courage to many a tormented soul. Yet the captains and dragoons feared this elusive figure while at the same time determining to place his head on the Netherbow. Many faithful Presbyterians were murdered on the spot or threatened with a touch of the thumbscrew or a place on the rack if they did not disclose the hiding place of some sought-out Covenanters.

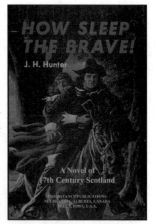

Lady Marion Kennedy, the beautiful daughter of the Lord of Culzean Castle, was also threatened with similar reprisals if she refused to marry Luis Salvador de Ferrari, the usurper of Fenwick Ha', and supporter of the Inquisition. Yet her heart longed for Duncan Fenwick, the rightful lord of Fenwick Ha'.

An exciting, fast-paced historical novel regarding the events of Scottish history in 1688.

Time: 1685-1688   Age: 12-99
ISBN 978-1-894666-41-1   Can.$15.95 U.S.$15.95

A Loyal Huguenot Maid
by Margaret S. Comrie
Huguenot Inheritance Series #8

Azerole, a young fugitive, was serving at Castle Brianza at Piedmont as governess to Madame de Rohan's crippled and plaintive foster son Christophe. But Azerole was a Huguenot maid, and Castle Brianza was ardently Roman Catholic. Madame's son Gaston, who was serving in the French army, was said to be a fiery Roman Catholic and tolerated no Protestants. What would happen to Azerole when he came home?

Azerole and her brother Léon struggle amid many troubles to keep their faith alive. When Michel unexpectedly comes on the scene a new unforseen danger lurks in the shadows. Would these two young Huguenots remain safe under the roof and shadow of Castle Brianza?

Time: 1686-1690 **Age: 12-99**
ISBN 978-0-921100-68-3 **Can.$15.95 U.S.$15.95**

Roger the Ranger by Eliza F. Pollard
A Story of Border Life Among the Indians

Indians, Frenchmen, Englishmen, wars, strained friendships, and romance are all interwoven in Eliza Pollard's fast paced historical novel.

When Charles Langlade deserted his birth place in upper Canada to marry an Indian squaw and then to fight with his Indian tribe for the French against

the English, he also lost his best friend, Roger Boscowen, who led his rangers for the English against the French.

Meanwhile the historically famous General Louis de Montcalm entered Canada on behalf of the French and things took a turn in favour for the French due to the help of Langlade. But would the jealous government of French Canada succeed in using De Montcalm's daughter Mercedes — who had come with her father from France with the intention to enter a Canadian convent — to destroy Montcalm's fame?

And would Charles and Roger indeed fight each other? Would their friendship ever be restored?

Time: 1754-1760 **Age: 12-99**
ISBN 978-1-894666-31-2 **Can.$14.95 U.S.$14.95**

Thea B. Van Halsema

Three Men Came to Heidelberg & Glorious Heretic: the Story of Guido de Brès
by Thea Van Halsema

From the sixteenth-century Protestant Reformation came two outstanding statements of faith: The Heidelberg Catechism (1563) and the Belgic Confession (1561). The stories behind these two historic documents are in this small book.

Frederick, a German prince, asked a preacher and a professor to meet at Heidelberg to write a statement of faith that would help teach his people the truths of the Bible. The result was the Heidelberg Catechism.

The writer of the Belgic Confession was a hunted man most of his life. Originally he wrote the confession as an appeal to the King of Spain to have mercy on the Protestants he was persecuting in the Lowlands. Not only was the request denied, but for his efforts the brilliant heretic de Brès was imprisoned and hanged by the Spanish invaders.

Time: 1556-1587   Age: 12-99
ISBN 978-1-894666-89-3   Can.$9.95 U.S.$9.95

Trust God, Keep the Faith
by Bartha Hill - de Bres

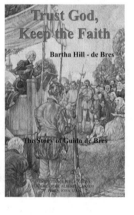

During the late sixteenth century the Reformation was sweeping across Europe. As the Bible became a loved book by the common man, many people questioned the beliefs and practices of the Roman Catholic Church at the perils of their lives. By torture and cruel deaths the priests attempted to return these "rebels" to the church.

In the midst of this battle Guido de Bres lived as he died — trusting God and keeping the faith.

Nearly five hundred years have passed since he was born, but the confession of faith written by Guido de Bres — a wonderful summary of God's Word — continues to live on in the lives of Reformed people around the world.

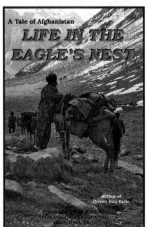

This book, written by one of his descendants, is about Guido de Bres. It describes the time in which he lived, and the confession of faith God allowed him to write.

Though intended for older children it also will be enjoyed by adults.

Time: 1522-1567   Age: 12-99
ISBN 978-0-921100-10-2   Can.$17.95 U.S.$17.95

Life in the Eagle's Nest by Charlotte Maria Tucker (A.L.O.E.)
A Tale of Afghanistan

Go with Walter Gurney, the seventeen-year-old orphan son of a British missionary in India, who, after meeting handsome, boastful Dermot Denis, joined him on a trip into Afghanistan.

Subject: Mission / Fiction   Age: 11-99
ISBN 978-1-894666-29-9   Can.$11.95 U.S.$10.90

This Was John Calvin
by Thea Van Halsema

J.H. Kromminga: "Though it reads as smoothly as a well written novel, it is crammed with important facts. It is scholarly and popular at the same time. The book will hold the interest of the young but will also bring new information to the well informed. . . . This book recognizes the true greatness of the man without falling into distortions of the truth to protect that greatness."

John Calvin comes alive as the author brings imagination as well as research to bear upon her subject. Her portrayal of the Genevan reformer is both appealing and honest.

From this account, Calvin no longer is seen merely as "carved like a monument in the panorama of human history," but has become vivid, lifelike, and real. This is biography at its best.

This Was John Calvin has been translated into Spanish, Portuguese, Korean, Chinese, Indonesian, and Japanese. This is its fifth printing in English.

Time: 1509-1564   **Age: 12-99**
ISBN 978-1-894666-90-9   Can.$11.95 U.S.$11.95

Bobby's Friends
by Phia van den Berg

The publisher's most favourite juvenile story

Pakistan! Every year a part of Western Pakistan underwent a drastic flood, washing away all the gardens and homes of the inhabitants. Father Falois, agriculturist, was asked by the government to try to control the floods. But life in Pakistan was so different for Bobby and his siblings. The worst part was understanding the people, that breach between the rich Muslims and the poor Christians. How would Bobby find friends? Would the screaming, proud, millionaire's son, Sadiq, be a friend, or would Jahja, the very poorest of all? Who would be faithful when danger came?

Subject: Fiction   **Age: 9-99**
ISBN 9780921100515   Can.$9.95 U.S.$9.95

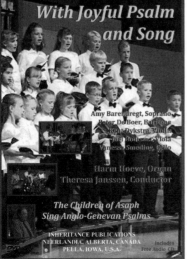

DVD (with FREE AUDIO CD)
With Joyful Psalm and Song

The Children of Asaph
Sing Anglo-Genevan Psalms
Amy Barendregt, Soprano
Peter De Boer, Baritone
Kent Dykstra, Violin
Joel Bootsma, Viola
Vanessa Smeding, Cello
Harm Hoeve, Organ
Theresa Janssen, Conductor

Psalms 76:1, 3, & 5; 93:1-4; 85:1 & 2; 114:1-4; 35:1 & 2; 6:1 & 2 (Soprano Solo); 47:1-3; The Song of Mary; Psalms 33 (Organ Solo); 79:1, 3, & 5; 89:1-3; 119:1, 4, 13, & 40; 24:1, 2, & 5; 144:2 (Strings & Baritone); 84:1-3; 55:1, 2, & 9; 71:1 & 8; 138:1-4.

IPDVD 113-9 (includes free CD)   **$29.95**

John Calvin: Genius of Geneva
by Lawrence Penning
A Popular Account of the Life and Times of John Calvin

Penning shows the Life of Calvin against the turbulence, religious unrest, and intellectual ferment of the times, when Europe stormed with Reformation and Counter Reformation, and traces the incredible full life and work of the man who was not only the greatest of the of the sixteenth century Reformers, but who was the greatest man of his age. Here we see too, the man Calvin: a man of infinite tenderness as well as of great temper; one who despised money for himself, but who thought it very important when counseling a friend entertaining thoughts of marriage.

Time: 1509-1564   Age:15-99
ISBN 1-894666-77-1   Can.$19.95 U.S.$16.90

Against the World - The Odyssey of Athanasius
by Henry W. Coray

Muriel R. Lippencott in *The Christian Observer*: [it] . . . is a partially fictionalized profile of the life of Athanasius . . . who died in A.D. 373. Much of the historical content is from the writing of reliable historians. Some parts of the book, while the product of the author's imagination, set forth accurately the spirit and the temper of the times, including the proceedings and vigorous debates that took place in Alexandria and Nicea. . . This is the story that Rev. Coray so brilliantly tells.

Time: A.D. 331-373   Age: 16-99
ISBN 0-921100-35-3   Can.$8.95 U.S.$7.90

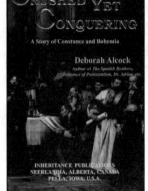

Crushed Yet Conquering
by Deborah Alcock

A gripping story filled with accurate historical facts about John Huss and the Hussite wars. **Hardly any historical novel can be more captivating and edifying than this book.** Even if Deborah Alcock was not the greatest of nineteenth century authors, certainly she is our most favourite.
— Roelof & Theresa Janssen

Time: 1414-1436   Age: 11-99
ISBN 1-894666-01-1   Can.$19.95 U.S.$16.90

Hubert Ellerdale by W. Oak Rhind
A Tale of the Days of Wycliffe

Christine Farenhorst in *Christian Renewal*: Christians often tend to look on the Reformation as the pivotal turning point in history during which the Protestants took off the chains of Rome. This small work of fiction draws back the curtains of history a bit further than Luther's theses. Wycliffe was the morning star of the Reformation and his band of Lollards a band of faithful men who were persecuted because they spoke out against salvation by works. Hubert Ellerdale was such a man and his life (youth, marriage, and death), albeit fiction, is set parallel to Wycliffe's and Purvey's.

Rhind writes with pathos and the reader can readily identify with his lead characters. This novel deserves a well-dusted place in a home, school, or church library.

Time: 1380-1420   Age: 13-99
ISBN 0-921100-09-4   Can.$12.95 U.S.$10.90

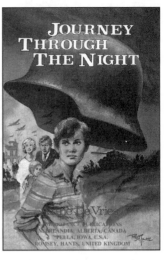

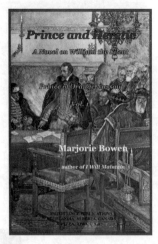

Prince and Heretic
by Marjorie Bowen
A Novel on William the Silent vol. 1

"The mind and the soul are not in the keeping of king nor priest — no man has a lordship over another man's conscience. All history has proved that." —William of Orange

Here is a fascinating historical novel for teenagers and adults about one of the greatest heroes of all time. William of Orange, considered today the father of Europe (and who can also fittingly be called the step-father of North America and the whole free western world) sets the stage as stadtholder of the Roman Catholic King of Spain, Philip II. William, though a nominal Roman Catholic at the time, determines to help the persecuted Protestants and in the process marries the Protestant Princess Anne of Saxony. But will Anne truly be a helpmeet for her husband? When he is pressed to take up the sword against King Philip he does not hesitate. In his struggles, William not only finds the God of his mother but grows in courage and the conviction that God has chosen him to be a faithful instrument to gain freedom for Christ's Church. William sacrifices all his possessions to pay the hired soldiers, but is it of any use? His brothers, Lodewyk, John, Adolphus, and Henry, also give all they have for the cause of freedom of a country which can hardly be called their own. Behind these heroes, a faithful praying mother, Juliana of Stolberg, waits for news at the German castle of Dillenburg.

Time: 1560-1568   Age: 13-99
ISBN 978-0-921100-56-0   Can.$17.95 U.S.$17.95

110726

William by the Grace of God
by Marjorie Bowen
A Novel on William the Silent vol. 2

The sequel to *Prince and Heretic*, by Marjorie Bowen.

King Philip II of Spain is prepared to make any concession to the lowlands, except freedom of conscience and worship and thus William of Orange continues in the struggle for true liberty. More important noblemen and personal friends sacrifice their lives, leaving few of William's original friends alive. But Charlotte de Bourbon is ready to encourage her hero despite all the crises he must endure. When Leyden is under siege William becomes ill. Will the cause have to be given up?

King Philip, in the meantime, is furious because he cannot get rid of William. Everyone on his black list is dead but

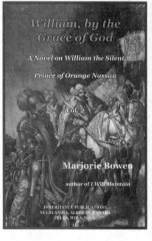

not the most important one: William of Orange. In a fury he writes the Ban and publishes it abroad. With this permission to dispose of his enemy in any way, the King is sure someone will kill William for him. After all, they will receive a great reward: a high position and name, wealth, fame . . . Will King Philip's plan succeed?

Time: 1569-1584   Age: 13-99
ISBN 978-0-921100-57-7   Can.$17.95 U.S.$17.95